Little
DOZEN
press

Exile

Published by Little Dozen Press
Stevensville, Ontario, Canada
www.littledozen.com

Cover design by Mercy Hope
Copyright 2013

ISBN: 978-0-9880613-7-8

EXILE

by Rachel Starr Thomson

Little Dozen Press

2013

"There's someone in the net—Tyler, haul the net in!"

Dark clouds were billowing over a choppy sea, the boat charging up and down the waves, when the words sank in. Through the spray and the looming storm Tyler saw it too— an arm, a flash of shoe. He braced himself and hauled, every muscle in his arms and back straining, and Chris joined him, still shouting:

"Pull!"

The wind gusted and pushed them like a thing alive.

They got the net over the rail and dumped it on the deck, silver fish flapping, detritus, and the person—a girl—a woman, young. Alive.

Tyler's eyes darted to the cliffs a mile off. "Did you fall?" he screamed over the wind.

She shook her head, hugging herself, gathering her feet beneath her. Long hair, water-dark, clung to her face and neck.

"I jumped," she said.

"Why the—" he started to swear, but one look at her hollow, tormented grey eyes shut his mouth.

* * * * *

The rain had just begun to fall from black clouds when they finished tying up the boat safe in the cove and began the trudge up the cliff path to the cottage—not that it mattered much to the boys, spray soaked as they were, and their guest seemed to feel nothing, see nothing.

An hour later she sat cross-legged on the ratty plaid couch in the side room, surrounded on three sides by big, screened windows that showed the sweeping cliffs, sky, and clouds. The bay seemed far off and far below, farther than it really was. Stacks of ragged paperbacks and a few board games in cardboard boxes sat beneath the low windowsills, wearing permanent impressions in the brown shag carpet.

She wore jeans and a button-up shirt that belonged to Tyler—he was the smaller of the two—and had a fuzzy flannel blanket, dull green, wrapped around her shoulders.

The electric heater in the corner of the room creaked and seemed to settle its feet. Tyler pressed a steaming mug of tea into her hands.

As her fingers tightened around it, her eyes met his. The same pain that had punched his anger away on the boat was still there, making him wince, but this time there was an openness there too—and a reaching, a plea. For a moment. Then it switched off, and she retreated again behind the pain.

Like a film over her eyes, Tyler thought.

He cleared his throat. "Hope that'll warm you—get the rest of the chill out."

She nodded. She had showered, and with a plastic comb of Chris's had patiently worked all the tangles out of her long, straight hair, which was drying to a dark blonde. Despite the shower and the blanket and the heater radiating too-strong electric heat, she still looked cold.

"Thank you," she said.

Rain beat against the windows in a sudden assault. Tyler settled awkwardly on the ottoman across from the couch, displacing a couple of fishing magazines. He leaned forward with his elbows on his knees and clasped his hands in front of him.

You weren't supposed to leave suicidal people alone, right? And Chris was doing the laundry.

"You're, ah . . . you're welcome."

A click and more settling from the heater.

The question just jumped out. "You lose someone?"

Something flickered in her eyes. "I lost . . . yeah."

"A husband?" Another flicker—deeper pain. He kicked himself inwardly. Idiot.

But she said, "No."

Tyler took a deep breath and wished he'd made a second cup of tea. Not that she was drinking hers—she was just holding it while it steamed between her hands.

"Well, somebody must be looking out for you," he charged in again. She shot him a look, but he just kept going. "To survive that fall in the first place . . . and then for us to pull you out like that, in the whole bay to be in just the right place, and with a storm comin' in . . ."

He shook his shaggy head. "Somebody didn't want you to die today."

When he looked up from his speech, she had turned her head and was staring out the wall of windows toward the sea. One arm rested on the back of the couch, and she was covering her mouth with the heel of her hand. The tea sat nestled in her lap.

His heart did an awful sort of plunge, and he swallowed hard and stood up. His throat hurt. "I'll come . . . check on you. Later."

The room was an add-on. Tyler stepped through the old side door into what had once been a mudroom but now housed a washer and dryer, an old dog kennel, a pile of fishing nets, and lots of unclaimed clothing—coats, boots, old socks without partners. He concentrated, for a moment, on breathing.

Cripes. It wasn't supposed to be this hard. Still.

Chris poked his head and big shoulders through the kitchen door. Unlike Tyler's unruly head of long blond curls and ever-present scruff, Chris's red hair was neat and short and his face clean shaven. At the moment he looked concerned.

"How's the patient?"

"Warming up," Tyler managed.

"You left her alone?"

"She needs space."

"But what if she—"

"She's not going to hurt herself. She just . . . it's grief, Chris. She lost somebody. She needs space."

Chris looked unconvinced. "I'm calling Mum."

"Yeah, okay. Good idea."

The kitchen door shut, and Tyler heard the sounds of Chris dialing from the other side. Trapped between worlds, suspended in the mudroom for a couple of minutes, Tyler waited.

Thunder rumbled, and the rain drummed on the roof.

* * * * *

With windows on three sides that covered nearly the whole wall from a foot above the floor to just below the low, sloping ceiling, Reese felt enveloped by the storm. Black, tumultuous clouds. Forked lightning; thunder that shook the walls. Pelting rain. It was a classic coastal storm, wind slamming the cliffs and churning the sea in a white frenzy she could just see from here, despite the darkness.

Bitter tears ran down her face, but she hardly noticed them. Her eyes were perpetually swollen and tender; light hurt them. Had ever since the . . . since the loss.

She stood by the window, placed a hand on the glass. Thunder cracked, and the glass strained against the wind howling up the cliff and battering the cottage.

Surrounded by the storm—except that she stood behind windows, in the warmth, smelling the faint burnt smell of an old heater, wrapped up and clean and dry except for her hair.

She was done with miracles. But perhaps they weren't done with her.

She sighed and leaned her head against the window like it was too heavy to hold up on her own.

Something made her open her eyes.

She saw it coming and jumped back an instant before the huge, black thing shattered the window and went straight for her throat.

* * * * *

Diane Sawyer's tea kettle was just starting to whistle, the high-pitched sound joining the thunder. She pinched the phone between her ear and shoulder, freeing both her hands to switch off the gas and lift the copper kettle off the burner.

"She what? I'm sorry, son, the thunder . . . yes. I heard you that time. Well, that's a little hasty, don't you think?" Steam wet her hand as she poured the water into the old ceramic pot, and she stuck her fingers sideways into her mouth to suck off the burn.

She frowned. "You don't know that, Christopher."

She switched the phone to her other ear, relieving the crick in her neck. "Mm-hmm. Yes, I'll come. But you'd probably be best off just—"

A sound like mirrors smashing came from the other end of the line, Chris swore, and Diane said "Christopher? What's going on?" just as an image loomed fully formed in her mind's eye, blacking out all other vision and sound for an instant. When she came back to her kitchen, she realized Chris had hung up.

She grabbed her purse, tea forgotten. Storm or no storm, she had to get up to the cottage.

* * * * *

Reese stood in the midst of the shattered glass, breathing hard and staring at the object in her hand. Behind her, first Tyler and then Chris tumbled into the side room.

"What is that?" Tyler blurted, pointing at the corpse on the floor, at the same time that Chris demanded, "Why are you holding a sword?"

Why indeed? She'd not thought to hold one ever again.

"Didn't think I . . . could," she offered, aware that her trailing answer wouldn't make sense to them. She nudged the thing on the floor with her toe and winced at the broken glass everywhere.

One more mess. The creature was only a renegade—thank God. But . . .

The sword disappeared, disintegrating into nothing, and she let her hand fall to her side. "I'm sorry about the mess."

Tyler lurched forward and kicked at the body, turning it over. He blinked. "It's a bat? But . . ."

Rain was blowing in through the broken window, spattering the piles of old books and quickly damping the carpet. Reese sprang into action, shuffling things aside and apologizing again. Night was falling, and it was dark. The wind through the window was cold.

Exile 11

Chris appeared at her side with a blue tarp, which he nailed over the windowsill with a few expert whacks of a hammer. With that little bit of a rain barrier in place, he stood back, regarded Reese with his arms folded over his chest, and said, "Who are you?"

She was still repositioning stacks of books, studiously avoiding looking at either of them. But she couldn't just ignore the question. "My name is Reese," she said.

"You have a last name?"

"No, we—I—we don't use them," she stammered. Why wouldn't the words come out? His gaze was boring into her, and she dropped what she was doing and sat on the couch again, shoulders hunched, bone weary. Of course she needed a last name.

"Danby," she let out in a whimper. "You can . . . Danby."

She ventured a glance up. Chris was still staring at her, but although his gaze was stern, she could see now that it wasn't angry. It was . . . protective, maybe.

The lump in her throat suddenly grew until all she wanted to do was curl up on the couch, cover herself with the flannel blanket, and give vent to all she felt until she had exhausted every tear and more, until every muscle ached and her skin burned with the emptiness inside.

His anger would have been hard to take. But protectiveness was a memory, too fresh and far, far too potent.

"A bat couldn't have broken that window—and I could have sworn it was something else, something way bigger when I walked in here. So what was that?"

Tyler wasn't paying attention to the exchange, and his question, to her relief, deflected the force of her grief. She considered lying, but she was too tired for that. She leaned back against the scratchy plaid upholstery.

"A renegade," she said. "Just one . . . so you don't need to worry that others will come."

Outside, headlight beams came around a curve in the road just below the cottage, disappearing behind the tarp after only a brief flash.

"That'll be Mum," Chris said. He frowned. "I think I hung up on her."

"A renegade?" Tyler pressed.

"Do you believe in demons?" Reese asked.

Chris shook his head. His forehead was creased with worry. "I'll put tea on," he said. "Wait this conversation. Until Mum's in here."

Tyler looked apologetically at Reese. "Diane is good for this kind of thing."

Reese felt the slightest glimmer of humour. "For discerning crazy?"

Tyler gave her a wry smile. "For helping us know what to do." He stood, leaving the bat he had been examining on the floor. "I don't think it's going to get any warmer and drier in here tonight. We'd better go to the living room."

He escorted Reese through a cluttered laundry room and a small kitchen, equally cluttered but surprisingly clean, where Chris was putting another kettle on. On the other side of the kitchen counter was a tiny room almost entirely occupied by a couch and an easy chair. One wall was swallowed up by a fireplace, over which hung a massive sword—a claymore, Reese thought. A small fire was going, and the room was warm.

She closed her eyes for a second. That only two hours ago she had thrown herself off a cliff in a vain attempt to drown herself seemed about as far away and unreal as hope. Strange how life could hang on and continue even when she didn't want it to—stranger that it could bring her somewhere like this, now.

And the sword. Why had the sword come to hand?

The rain nearly masked the sound of a car pulling up outside the cottage, and in a moment the front door pushed open and a woman stumbled in, wrapped in a sleek rain slicker and wearing a kerchief which she promptly pulled off and wrung out. She was short and comfortably built, and her pale hair was twisted in a French knot at the back of her head. Her sharp eyes fixed on Reese immediately.

"So you're the girl," she said. "I'm Diane. How are my boys treating you?"

Reese stammered something . . . even she wasn't sure what words she was trying to say. Mercifully, Tyler and Chris both began to talk, telling this woman—Chris's mother, Diane—what had happened, from the rescue right down to the demon that had turned into a bat and the sword that had appeared and then dematerialized in Reese's hand. Getting out of her rain slicker and boots, Diane listened intently and nodded, without interrupting or appearing surprised at any point.

Finally she crossed the tiny room and took Reese's arm. Her hands were weathered and heavy veined, older than the rest of her, and cold from the drive through the rain.

"Sit," she said. "I think we should all sit."

They did. Chris and Tyler looked uncomfortable, and after about half a second Chris stood up again and positioned himself in front of the fireplace. His mother didn't chastise him.

"I saw it," she said without any more preamble. "The demon. I see things sometimes—the boys know. That's how I knew to get up here fast."

She peered along her nose at Reese. Her eyes were blue. "And you," she said. "You are a part of the Oneness."

For an instant Reese thought she would not find her voice, or even the breath to say it. But she did—somehow she did.

"No," she said. "No, I'm an exile."

"A what?" Chris said. "A ... from what?"

Diane ignored her son, instead keeping her eyes fixed on Reese. Compassion, crushing with the weight of the girl's words, flooded her. The haunted eyes, the obvious grief, the plunge into the sea—it all made sense now. But there was more to this than one young woman's grief, and Diane found that deep within, she quivered.

How was it even possible? The Oneness couldn't separate—couldn't break.

Could it?

But surely if it wasn't true, this girl would know it. And she wouldn't be a living icon of loss.

Diane's practicality and her heartache on the girl's behalf crowded out her other dominant emotion—resentful unhappiness that somehow, she was mixed up in this.

The boys, of course, had no idea what this was all about.

Best friends who had bought the old cliff cottage together and determined to waste their best years fishing in the bay, they were good-hearted and as purely earthy as the fishing nets, woven of hemp and smelling forever of seaweed, that they spent their days up to their knees in. The Oneness was not part of any world they had ever brushed against.

Chris was the image of his father: all brawn and sea and seriousness. He was too young when Douglas died to remember him but had grown into his likeness all the same. Tyler, now—Tyler knew what grief was. Something about Reese must have brought it back, because Diane had spotted it in his eyes when she arrived—that look he'd worn on his face for two years, his tenth to twelfth, after his parents died in the accident.

But no, the boys knew nothing about the world to which Reese belonged—or had belonged. It was her unspoken agreement with Chris: when the supernatural came knocking, she dealt with it and left him out of it as much as possible.

He couldn't be happy about this.

Not that he would make the girl leave. Not her son. She knew Chris—he was just like his father. Now that Reese had been under his care for even a few hours, he would put himself in death's way before he would leave her defenceless.

If she had truly been exiled from the Oneness, who knew what that natural bent would cost Douglas Sawyer's son?

Diane covered her face with her hands and stifled a groan.

Tyler, thankfully, wasn't done with his questions. "You said demons," he said, looking at Reese. "You asked if I believe in demons."

"Yes," Reese said. She sounded weary. Clearly he wanted her to go on, but she didn't—so he cleared his throat and continued.

"I don't know. Maybe I do. Now. I saw that thing before it . . . turned into a bat. Right? Is that what happened?"

"Yes," Chris said, his voice tight. "That's what happened. After she stabbed it."

"Are you an angel?" Tyler asked.

Diane started to interject, to cut off Tyler's unfortunately ignorant questions, but to her surprise, Reese answered.

"No."

"What is the Oneness?" Chris asked.

This time Reese didn't answer. More than likely she couldn't. Diane wrestled with the combination of compassion, anger, and fear that had been assailing her since Chris's phone call, and which heightened with every moment she spent in this lost child's presence.

"They are a force," Diane said. "One of three spiritual forces in this world. We've already named the first two."

"Angels and demons," Tyler said. "Everyone knows about those. Why haven't I ever heard of this . . . this . . ."

"Because the Oneness is the most important of the three," Diane answered. "And thus the most hidden."

"Come on," Tyler said, leaning back, his eyes widening. "More than angels?"

Reese found her voice. "Angels are just messengers," she said. "And servants. Who do you think they serve?"

"God," Tyler promptly answered.

Reese ventured a faint smile. "Well, yes. Everything does. But more . . . specifically, angels are servants to us."

She caught herself, and the smile vanished completely. "To them."

Tyler opened his mouth to ask another question, but Diane jumped in. This conversation could go on all night, and she wasn't sure they had the time. She was sure Reese didn't have the desire, or likely the stamina, for it either. She thought of trying to soften her questions but decided that quick was merciful.

"What was that demon doing here if you're not part of the Oneness anymore?"

"I'm not . . . it was a renegade. Not part of an organized force. Most likely it was just going for a joy kill."

"Stupid," Chris said. Diane raised her eyebrows. He was quick, her kid—too quick for his own good. He clarified: "To act as a renegade—to work against the best interests of the whole force like that."

"They are a house divided. That's why they will lose," Reese said.

"But you had a sword," Diane continued. "Chris said he saw one in your hand."

Reese looked at the floor between her hands. "I don't know why that happened. Apparently I haven't . . . haven't lost everything yet."

The words were barely out of her mouth before there were tears tracking down her face. Diane sighed and stood, putting a motherly hand to Reese's hair. "So you're sure there's no more threat? Nothing is coming after you tonight?"

Reese's voice was misery itself. "It's not likely, but I can't make promises. I don't know what another renegade might do."

Chris stepped forward, the claymore above the fireplace a suitable backdrop to his big-shouldered frame. "Good, then," he said. "You can take my bed for the night—I'll sleep out here."

"I—all right."

Diane saw the raw gratitude that flashed in the girl's eyes. Her son had better watch his step. He was a fine, good-looking, strong young man, and this girl was vulnerable.

And dangerous.

* * * * *

"Well?" Chris asked.

Tyler and Reese had retired to opposite corners of the house. Diane stayed by the flickering fire, warming her feet. They hadn't warmed since she entered the cottage. Chris had disappeared for a little while, rummaging around in his room for blankets and a pillow, which he dumped on the couch before crossing his arms and regarding his mother with an air of expectation.

So much like Douglas.

"Well what?" Diane asked.

"All that stuff she said about the Oneness being a force and like angels . . . servants of God."

"All true. There are more things in heaven and earth, my boy, than most of us have ever dreamt of."

"But what is it . . . this Oneness thing? That girl in my room—is she some kind of angel or ghost or . . ."

"No, no," Diane said, shaking her head. "She's as human as we are. The Oneness is people. But more than people, too."

"Why haven't I ever heard of them?"

Diane shrugged. "They're hidden."

"Because they're treacherous?"

"Because they're plain." Diane reflected a moment. "I have never met one who was trying to hide. Hidden in plain sight—you've heard that saying? The Oneness is like that. Angels and demons are mysterious, terrifying, beautiful—supernatural. So we talk about them. But the Oneness are just there. They're hidden because no one thinks they're worth paying attention to, except once in a while when they . . ."

Her eyes clouded over for a moment at a memory—a family huddled in her kitchen, fleeing the rancour of men. It had been Douglas who brought them home. Douglas, the unbeliever, who insisted they hide them. Douglas who turned their pursuers away.

And Douglas who was undone by them. By their love for each other.

Their oneness.

". . . when they get in the way," she finished lamely.

"So they're just people," Chris said. "Then why are they any different from you or me?"

Diane gazed into her son's face and saw her husband there again. "Do you know the story of Babel?" she asked.

He frowned and scratched his nose. "Rings a bell."

"The Tower of Babel," Diane prompted. "Old story . . . one of the oldest. It's in the Bible."

He shook his head. "Don't think I know it."

"Thousands of years ago, near the beginning of time, all mankind got together to build a tower to heaven," Diane said. "It was to be a monument to them and lift them into the very presence of God. But it was an affront to him too, because their hearts were rebellious and evil. Nevertheless, they started their building. And God looked down and said, 'The people are one, and behold, nothing they set out to do will be impossible for them.'"

Chris looked confused. "Go on."

"So God took it upon himself to stop them. He came down to the Tower of Babel disguised as a man, and he cursed the people so their tongues became confused. Where before they had all spoken the same language, now their speech became gibberish in one another's ears. Without the ability to understand one another, the people were forced to separate, and they scattered themselves across the face of the whole earth."

"Interesting story," Chris said.

Diane managed a thin smile. "There is another story. Not so many people know this one."

He smiled back—a big, generous smile. "But you do."

"Mankind never did build his tower to heaven. Many years—thousands of years—later, a man from heaven built a ladder to earth. He promised to send the Spirit to earth, to work a miracle in all who wait to receive it. His followers gathered together in a room and waited for that Spirit to descend. Suddenly, they all began to speak in languages they had never known before, and every one of them understood every other."

"A reversal," Chris said.

"Exactly. And the Oneness was born."

"How long ago was that?" Chris asked, clearly sceptical.

"No one knows for sure—a few thousand years, give or take."

Chris leaned back against the couch and folded his arms across his big chest. "Uh-huh. What do they do?"

Diane paused, her mind flipping through hundreds of still images, conversations, insights. "I think—"

She smiled and spread out her hands, beseeching Chris to believe her.

"I think they hold the world together."

* * * * *

It rained all night, and when the sun rose, it cast its golden, rosy light on a wet, glistening world. April watched it come up from her perch on the rooftop, looking down over the sharply sloping streets to the neighbourhood and the harbour at the base of the cliff.

She heard the sound of a window being pushed open and a grunt as Richard climbed out of the second-story lookout. He made his way gingerly across the shining shingles and sat down next to April, handing her a warm travel mug.

She took a sip. Coffee. Nice and strong.

"Thanks."

"No problem. You see anything?"

April turned her eyes back to the bright horizon, light shining off the bay waters beyond the town, and tried to scan the streets. The sun in her eyes made their gloom harder to penetrate. "Not yet."

They made an odd couple—the six-foot-two black man with a neatly trimmed beard and close-shaved hair, wearing a suit, and the five-foot-two blonde with her hair in a ponytail and a blanket swathed around her shoulders.

The coffee warmed her quickly, and she shed the blanket. The sun warmed her bare shoulders and brightened the rose-vine tattoo inked across her right. She wore a tank top and track pants and sneakers. Ready to run.

Richard twined his fingers and pushed them outward, cracking his knuckles. "I gotta go to work. Mary's coming with breakfast. You need anything else?"

"Naw. I'll be fine." She turned and met his eyes, smiled brightly. His care emanated back at her, warming her like the sun, and he smiled at her smile.

"Good day at work," she said.

"Thanks. You take care."

"Of course. I'm ready for anything."

"You know what pride comes before."

"All right, almost anything. But I'm not alone. So I'll be fine."

He grinned and pushed himself back up, careful of his

footing. She laughed at the wet shingle debris clinging to the back of his suit.

"Brush off!"

"You got it!"

She turned her eyes back to the streets as Richard left. It was still hard to see, but what she was looking for would stand out. To her, anyway.

There were a multiplicity of gifts in the Oneness, no two exactly alike. April had eyes to see.

There. She saw the glint of metal, the mad pedalling, and the desperation.

Right on time.

The boy was only about a block away, flying down a narrow, cobbled street toward the glimmering waters of the harbour. He would be almost impossible to catch. Which was fine, because she didn't need to catch him. She only needed to follow.

April disdained the window and stairs; traipsing through the house would take too much time. She cast off her blanket completely and abandoned the travel mug in the eaves trough where it wouldn't roll away; grabbing the drainpipe with a gloved hand, she slid down and landed hard on the soft earth. Her legs were moving almost before she'd fully landed. To run. There was nothing like it.

It was a quick sprint over level ground for fifty yards before she plunged downhill on the street leading through town. The run turned to a jog, her whole body jarring as she tried to outwit gravity and stay on her feet. The town before her still shone in the rising sun.

The boy on the bike disappeared over a second downhill plunge, and April picked up her speed, regaining sight of him just as he rode straight into the little cluster of fishing shacks and boathouses at the centre of the harbour. Beyond them, the sun was still rising. But this boy had been swallowed instead by shadows.

It took her ten minutes to reach the gloomy little huddle of huts. The sky overhead was clear and the bay calm; the storm had vanished as storms always did. But here it was dark, shadows extending from the closely constructed buildings. Boat masts stuck up behind them, bobbing slightly.

"Hello?" April called, worming her way between a couple of especially tight shacks. The bike lay abandoned outside them. The passage was narrow enough that she had to angle herself slightly to get through, and the slopes of both roofs met in the middle to plunge the space into shadow. Old plastic bottles and a gas can littered it. She could see a door on one side, closed, but definitely there.

She stared intently at it and saw a sparkle of light from beneath the door. Yeah, he was here.

With a tentative hand on the door handle, she called out again. "Anybody in there?"

No answer. She turned the handle and pushed.

The door opened easily. Inside, the shack was even gloomier than its side entranceway. One window, facing south, was covered with grime. It let in just enough light for April to make out the nets, stacks of lobster traps, and cases of bottled water stored in most of the shack's space.

The boy sat crammed between two stacks of water, cases

piled six high. His hair was blond and unruly, long enough to hang in his face. He was ten, maybe eleven. Maybe thirteen. April hadn't been able to guess his age, and she hadn't asked.

April took a step closer, holding out her hand like an offering. "Hey, Nick, are you okay?" she asked. Knowing full well he wasn't.

"What are you doing here?" he asked. His voice quavering.

"I saw you riding down here . . . thought you might ride right into the bay."

He smiled at that. "I'm a good rider."

"So," April asked, "you come here a lot?"

"Most days."

"What's the attraction?"

Nick shrugged. "It's quiet."

She let her eyes leave his face for a moment and noticed a stack of comic books shoved under the pallet of water. The space where he was sitting was less dusty, less cobwebbed, than most corners of the shack. Quiet. April thought of all the times she'd seen him tearing down here on his bike and wondered what kind of noise he was running from. Her own memories gave her plenty to work with—broken glass, shouting. The curses and the names. She grimaced. She'd excise it all in a heartbeat if she could—all of life before the Oneness. But Richard said her past was why she could see like she could—why, in this case, she was sensitive enough to know a boy fleeing and hiding when others thought he was just being a normal kid, flying down the hill for the sake of adrenaline.

She'd been reaching out to Nick for a couple of weeks now,

finding him loitering around the village and buying him soda or lunch or whatever. She'd have to add comic books to the list. He treated her warily, and she didn't ask him much about his life. Just talked to him and let him get comfortable in her presence.

"Listen, you had breakfast? You wanna go get some food?"

His eyes had that bright look in them. She spared him the need to answer and just reached out her hand.

He took it, and she pulled him to his feet.

* * * * *

They were waiting outside the fishing shack, silent and unmoving as mountains. One a big man, well over six feet and built like a hammer; the other smaller, grossly tattooed, impatient. They stood on either side of the narrow passage between shanties, where they couldn't be seen by anyone coming through.

April knew they were there a second before she stepped out—a shadow, a sound, something gave them away. She thrust a hand behind her to stop Nick and said very softly, "Get back in there now." She tried to follow suit, but the kid was too slow getting out of the way; the smaller man hooked her elbow and yanked. Her instincts blazed and she tried to turn on him, pulling on her arm and lashing out with her leg simultaneously, but there was no time; no room. She was out of the passageway, and Hammer-man landed a blow to the back of her head.

Diane hadn't slept much since her visit to the boys' cottage on Wednesday night. She'd found herself pacing the dark rooms of her house in the wee hours that night, unhappily contemplating memories and things she knew, things she had seen. Reese's face hung in the midst of all her thoughts, the misery in her eyes. Was it true? Could the Oneness be broken?

And if it could, what other disaster might follow?

Thursday passed in a blur of the same thoughts, the same worries. She didn't call the boys and they didn't call her. A brightish morning gave way to rain again at night, another night like the one when Reese had come, and drove Diane's mood deep into clouds and recollections she didn't want.

It stopped raining just half an hour or so before dawn, and Diane fell asleep at about the same time. When the sun rose she woke just enough to pull the curtains tight shut against it, and so it was nearly noon before she found herself in the kitchen, frying bacon, wondering how the boys were getting on and what their visitor meant and was going to mean.

It was always possible Reese would turn out to belong somewhere, to be heading somewhere, and she would just thank her rescuers and leave. But Diane knew it wasn't going to happen that way. Chris wouldn't allow it; he was too protective—he would insist on seeing her home, making sure she wasn't really just going off to try to harm herself again. And Tyler was too perceptive; he would see through her if she lied.

Besides, she didn't belong anywhere. Nowhere except with the Oneness, and if she was telling the truth, she could not go back to them.

And if she had somewhere to go, she would have gone yesterday already.

Diane sighed and leaned against the stove. She didn't really want to think about all this. She wanted the world to go on turning like it had for so many years, with nothing wrong, nothing calamitous about to come down on their heads.

But she knew better. Calamity is always hanging over our heads—all of us, every day. Something is always wrong. And she of all people knew that.

"Maybe it's all a mistake," she said out loud.

A knock on the back door startled her so badly she nearly knocked the frying pan off the stove. She switched the gas off and took the three steps across the tiny kitchen to the door.

"Yes?"

She didn't know the man standing on her doorstep, though she'd seen him around the village. He was tall, dark-skinned, trim. But she knew the woman standing beside him. Short, wiry, Diane's own age. Piercing grey eyes and white strands of hair highlighting darker locks. Diane closed her eyes for the barest of instants and saw the kitchen again, the family, Douglas hiding them, keeping them away from the mob hunting them down. A man and his wife, four children, and this woman, the man's sister.

"Hello, Mary," Diane said.

"I'm sorry to come without any warning," Mary answered. "This is Richard." She hesitated. "May we come in?"

Diane opened the door all the ~~way and st~~ood against it without a word. Mary nodded and led the way into the kitchen. The three of them took up the whole room. Their presence was oppressive—bigger than the people who created it. But Diane did not ask them to come further into the house.

"We need your help," Mary said.

Diane cleared her throat. "I thought you had eyes?"

"We do." It was Richard who answered. "That's why we've come. Her name is April. She went missing yesterday morning."

"Missing?" Diane choked.

Mary's expression was earnest and direct. "She went out on a job, one she said would only take her a couple of hours. She was supposed to be back in time for breakfast. She didn't come. We got worried and started looking for her yesterday evening."

"Seems a little rash to say she's missing," Diane said, knowing full well that Mary was never rash—that the Oneness did and said very little in haste. "Maybe she just wanted to get away."

"Things have been dark lately," Richard said. "We are all careful to stay connected and report back in time. April wasn't careless. We've looked all over town and can't find her."

Diane cleared her throat. For a fleeting second she had hoped that the boys' Reese and this April might be one and the same—but no, this girl had only been missing since yesterday morning, and Reese had left her cell, wherever it was, at least sixteen hours earlier—enough time for her to cast herself off the cliffs.

"So you're here because . . ."

"We wondered if you've seen anything," Mary said.

Diane started to shake her head. "Do you know a girl called Reese?"

Richard frowned. "No."

"Never mind," Diane said. "I don't think I can help you." She knew what she should tell them—that she'd seen a demon two nights ago, in a flash of vision, and seen its bat-body dead on the floor, slain by a girl who said she was an exile from the Oneness and should not even have the power to wield a sword. A girl who claimed the impossible and yet believed it so deeply she had tried to take her own life only a few hours before. But she couldn't say it. The girl was involved with Chris, and Chris was her son, and Chris didn't need to become mixed up with these people—to become enamoured with them like Douglas had.

Like she had.

So she said only, "I haven't seen anything. Surely one of your own can help you."

"Diane . . ." Mary reached out to lay a comforting hand on Diane's shoulder, but it wasn't comforting. Anything but. Never, never had this woman brought comfort—not her and not her people.

The Oneness held the world together. Diane knew that, and she treated them with respect because of it. Respect, but not welcome.

And yet, she had to know.

"What do you think happened to her . . . April?"

"We don't know," Mary answered. "But we're worried. Something feels very wrong. You feel it too, even if you won't admit it."

Diane bristled a little. "Is there any possibility—any chance she might just have left?"

Richard frowned. "What do you mean?"

"Maybe she wanted to leave."

He shook his head, his face betraying how abhorrent he found the idea. "Not possible."

"Isn't it?" Diane asked, pretending the comment was offhanded. "Doesn't anyone ever leave the Oneness? Don't you ever throw anyone out?"

Mary paled. "How could you suggest such a thing!"

Diane wasn't sure herself. She softened. "I'm sorry. I was just trying to say that maybe things aren't as bad as they seem. Maybe, after all, this girl just went off on her own for some reason."

"I wish I could believe that," Richard said, cutting Mary off before she could respond more explosively. Though Diane doubted he knew the history between the two women, he seemed to have picked up on the strained dynamic between them and was doing his best to calm it down and stay focused on the reason they were there—the missing girl, concern for whom was evident in his whole bearing. "But she was clear on when to be back, and April doesn't just go off on her own. She knows better."

Diane shook her head, but she was less combative now. She considered once more telling them about Reese, then decided to leave it alone. Things were bad enough—one girl exiled from the Oneness, another inexplicably gone—without her getting into the middle of it.

Still, she couldn't just send them away with nothing.

"If I see anything that might help, I'll tell you," she promised.

Mary nodded. "Thank you." Richard caught her eye and raised an eyebrow in a look that meant, "Shall we go?" She nodded.

Then she met Diane's eyes one more time. "Things are dark," she said. "Like Richard told you. Be careful. And if you need us—well, you know where to find us."

The words came out dry, cracked. "I know."

Diane watched them go, padding across the damp ground to a car that was shiny and new and probably Richard's. He seemed like a man with a good job and a good paycheck, the kind who would do well in the world if he wanted to. But he wouldn't—not when he was one of them.

"I hope she turns up soon!" Diane called out, adding a well-wish to the promise she'd made to contact them if she saw anything. And she meant it.

The Oneness weren't her enemies, she knew that.

But that didn't make her any less afraid.

* * * * *

Richard kept his eyes on the road as he drove back up the cliff road to the house, not looking his companion's way. But the air between them was thick all the same.

Just as he turned up the road that would take them home, he said, "You have a history with that woman."

"It's not just me," Mary said. "We all do. Couldn't you sense it?"

He was quiet a moment. "Yes, I suppose I could."

Mary sighed as she clenched and relaxed her hands, trying to let out some of the tension she'd been carrying from the minute April should have arrived and hadn't. "You know she didn't tell us everything."

"It's not like we could force a confession." He sounded unhappy about it.

"I believe her, though—when she said she'd tell us if she could help us. She knows something, but she doesn't really think it would help or she would tell."

He shook his head. "I've never met one like her before."

Mary was silent as they pulled into the driveway. She rested her hand on the door handle and thought back, letting the memories play out. "They're not common," she finally said. "But it's not without reason, how she is. I've wished a thousand times I could go back and change what happened, but . . ."

"You know that's not in your hands," he said gently, putting the car in park. "And right now we've got to concentrate on getting April back." Even as he said the words, his face seemed to age with worry. "What do you think happened to her, Mary?"

Mary shook her head, the creases around her mouth and eyes strained.

Things are dark, they had told Diane. They had not explained what they meant—why they were so sure April had not just gone off to get some time alone, or lost track of time and decided to stay somewhere. Things were happening that they could not explain, not only here in their little village overlooking the bay, but out in the wider world—the letters, the dreams, the unsettled sense of a storm building. They had been expecting an attack.

April was only a beginning. They had to find her, yes, but equally they had to find some way to understand what was happening—before the enemy could move in full force and find them defenceless. But neither voiced that now.

They sat in the car in silence, both with their eyes closed, feeling the pressure of a storm front coming.

* * * * *

April awoke to pain spiking through her head so badly that she rolled over onto her stomach and tried desperately not to be sick. It took a few disoriented minutes to realize she was lying on a hard, rough rock surface, and that her hands were tied.

It was dark.

Confused and still battling stabs of pain from the back of

her skull, she tried to sort out the last things she remembered. The fishing shack . . . the boy. Leaving. The view down the narrow passage and the sun on the other side, and then . . .

She remembered. Twisting herself around, she sat up and lowered her forehead to her knees, pulled up against her chest. For a moment when the first man had stepped around that corner, she'd thought she was back in her own childhood. That was her father stepping around the corner. The grab for her, the blow, were expected.

But she had been wrong; she'd realized that quickly. She didn't know these men. She still didn't know why they had attacked her, or why they had brought her here, or where here was.

She held her head very still, hoping to clear it, and listened. A trickle of water somewhere. The rocky surface beneath her was dry, thankfully, but the air was cold. It was dark. This was a cave, she decided. She had been tied up and dumped in a cave.

She tried to pull her wrists apart, but they were bound securely with something broad and inflexible that would hardly let her move her hands. Duct tape. A sound not far away caught her attention and she jerked her head up, regretting it immediately as flashes of light ignited in front of her eyes and pain took up a dance in her head. She bit her lip to keep from making a sound.

No other noises followed, and no one appeared in the darkness around her. But when the lights stopped flashing in her eyes, she realized that it wasn't completely dark in the cave—her senses were adjusting, and she could make out a crisscrossing pattern in the murk ahead of her. It was a door, she realized, a barred metal gate. This place wasn't just a cave; it was a prison.

Exile   39

Moving her head very slowly to avoid a repeat of the fantastic headache that waited to pounce, she figured out where the nearest cave wall was and scooted backwards until she could lean against it. The more awake she became, the more acutely she realized that she was alone. She swallowed a lump in her throat and said a prayer for grace.

April shivered. The air in here was cool, and her tank top and track pants offered little warmth. What was she doing here? She tried to remember the men's faces, but she had barely had a look at them. She was sure she had never seen them before. Were they just human? Was this all just some man-made plot—was she being trafficked or held for ransom or targeted for some serial crime?

She seriously doubted it.

The months leading up to this day had been strange, full of the sense that something was coming. A foreboding felt in the spirit long before the mind could catch up. Often it was April who could make sense of such feelings, who could name the threats and see how to combat them. But not this time. When she tried, she could only find murk—confusion and darkness. And it wasn't just her. Letters had come from other Oneness cells, speaking of trouble but unable to offer specifics. Mary's dreams had been nightmarish, all of them warning, warning, warning . . . but the warnings remained indistinct, so without clarity that no one could act on them. Richard, faithful Richard, had been staking himself out in prayer three times a day, late at night and early in the morning, but to no avail. There was nothing. Only the sense that something was coming.

April could only assume this was the first strike.

She pushed down a growing sense of dread. She knew the

enemy, the cruelty and hatred associated with everything they did. She refused to imagine what they might be planning to do with her. Imaginations like that bred fear; and fear was central to their power. She flexed her hand as much as possible within the tape, feeling for the latent presence of a sword.

The Oneness lived always at war. The enemy was real and persistently active; others could live with the illusion of peace and harmony in the world, but the Oneness could not. And yet, attacks were not common in the fishing village. The little cell was so tiny, so inconsequential, that it attracted scant attention. April, Richard, Mary: just three individuals serving in a tiny town on the edge of the bay. There was nothing remarkable about any of them.

So what am I doing here? April wondered.

Gingerly she leaned her head against the rock wall and closed her eyes.

She could hear waves, some distance away. The bay. She wasn't far from home, then.

She smiled faintly.

* * * * *

When Reese awoke on Friday morning, it was to the smell of bacon and eggs and coffee. These boys were surprisingly domestic, she thought; or maybe they were just bothering to be that way because she was here. The thought made her feel welcomed and cared for, and that sensation lingered a moment before the heaviness replaced it—the sorrow that threatened to choke her off and cripple her again.

She'd spent yesterday in a fog. They had left her alone. She'd slept most of the day—just refusing to wake up. She wanted to be dead. At the very least she could keep herself mostly unconscious.

She pushed off the blankets she'd pulled over herself sometime in the night—for a long time she hadn't been able to find the motivation, but eventually the cold won out—and pushed herself out of bed, her feet and legs heavy, her arms weighed down. Heaviest of all was her heart, like an anchor in the centre of her being, dragging her down to a watery depth where she didn't want to go.

In the living room a fire was flickering. It had been going the night before, too—she'd noticed it when she got up for a few minutes. She wondered if Chris had sat by it all night, thinking thoughts of his own. He intrigued her, and she sensed that she intrigued him, in some way that scared and comforted her all at once. She looked around for him, but he was gone. It was Tyler who stood over a skillet on the stove, enduring the spitting of grease.

He flashed her a quick smile, one that was tired like an older man's smile after the strain of a long day. His face and his long, curly hair were so boyish that the weariness of the smile seemed out of place. Reese recognized it all at once and felt bad for failing to do so the day before. Tyler's was a smile marked by loss, by grief. He knew the heaviness she felt now, though the degree of his loss was lesser than hers.

Or if not lesser, she corrected herself, guilty as she looked at him for judging him less bereaved than herself, at least different.

"Would you like some breakfast?" he asked. "It's hot. Coffee's on the counter there . . . help yourself."

She nodded distractedly and poured herself a cup. It was thick and black, with no cream in sight. She grimaced at the heavy, bitter taste but welcomed it anyway. Plates clacked as Tyler shuffled the eggs and bacon onto two of them and handed one across the counter. Just two plates. Chris was gone, then.

"I'm going out on the water in a bit," Tyler said after he'd eaten a couple of distracted mouthfuls. "Thought you might want to come along. Unless it's . . . I mean, unless the water is going to bother you."

Reese thought about that for a moment. Would it bother her? Just two days ago she had stood at the top of a cliff, looking down on the bay and a distant storm coming, and let her sorrow and her loss drive her off, down through the air, into the cold embrace of the bay and the darkness, into the end of her physical life now that all that truly mattered had already ended. But somehow she had risen.

And she was alive today. More alive than she had been at the top of that cliff.

No, she decided, the water wouldn't bother her.

Tyler dug out some more old clothes for Reese to wear on the boat, and while she changed into overalls and a button-up striped shirt, he washed up the dishes. He tossed her a coat and a pair of much-too-large boots, the gaping space filled as much as possible with several layers of thick socks, and looked her over critically. Deeming her nearly ready, he grabbed a floppy-brimmed hat from the laundry room and handed it over.

"Good," he said. "I think we're ready to go."

When they exited the side door onto the sloping gravel driveway with its sharp dip and overlook of the village and bay, the crunch of car tires met their ears, and Diane drove over the ledge a moment later. She exited the car looking furtive.

"Is Chris here?" she asked Tyler.

"No ma'am," he replied. "He went out early. Can I help you with something?"

Diane cast a look at Reese and quickly averted her eyes, sliding back into the car after the slightest hesitation. "No," she said. "But if you're in when he gets back, call me." She started her car and began to back into a turn.

Reese frowned.

There was something about this woman.

"We'll ride in the truck," Tyler said, heading for a grease-stained carport at the side of the cottage. "It's a bit of a hike down to the water."

Just a minute, Reese wanted to say. She stood frozen in indecision, wanting to run up to Diane's car, motion for her to roll down the window, and say, "What is it? What's going on? What aren't you telling me?" But she didn't. How could she? She didn't know these people . . . and she didn't belong here. Or anywhere.

But . . .

She had seen the demon.

The realization hit like a weight. Diane had seen the demon. It was one thing for an ordinary mortal to know about the Oneness. Some people did. But to see the demons, and not with her eyes—to see them from far away, in a vision, with eyes to see . . .

Reese gasped.

Diane finished turning her car around in the tight space and roared down the hill. Reese's eyes filled with tears as she watched her go.

A blue pickup truck pulled up beside her. "Ready to go?" Tyler asked.

They rode in silence down the steep hill, the vista around them breathtaking. There was nothing like this—sweeping cliffs, quaint village nestled at the base of them and climbing up the sides with neighbourhoods like stray creeper vines, the blue of the bay stretching away to the horizon and the blue of the sky pristine above it—in the city where Reese had always lived. She wondered if the beauty had something to do with why today, although she still carried a heart heavy as rusted iron, she did not want to kill herself.

But she cast a glance beside her at the young man driving the truck, his blue eyes on the road, his tousled hair wild, and knew it had more to do with him and with Chris. Their rescue had extended to more than simply fishing her out of the water. Their kindness and protection was permission to live—a safe place where she could feel, and feel acutely, and yet not need to run.

She looked down at her hands in her lap. She was going to have to leave—you didn't just show up and take advantage of strangers forever. They weren't the Oneness. If only . . .

She forced her thoughts off that tangent.

It didn't take long to reach the wharf, and Tyler had the boat out with ease. The day was calm, beautiful. He worked the sail with muscled arms and spoke not a word to Reese. She sensed he was waiting for permission.

Briefly, she considered giving it.

The wind in her face was cold, but the sun shone down with warmth, glancing off the water beneath them in bursts of light. Reese could see why he loved the water. She wondered about his own story. Why he and Chris lived here when most young men their age would be heading for the city, or going to school, or trying to build some kind of career for themselves. Why Tyler smiled like an old man who knew grief. Why they were both so gentle and good.

And why Chris's mother was part of the Oneness and refused to admit it.

The painful lump was back in Reese's throat, and she swallowed it down again. Even when she tried to think about someone else, her thoughts always came back here. Back to the Oneness, to her family, to her love. The love from which she was now and forever outcast.

She looked at her hands and another question flickered in her thoughts. Why had she still been able to wield the sword when the demon attacked?

Why had it attacked at all?

Demons were petty. Most likely the attack was nothing but spite. It saw her wounded, alone, and thought to finish her off.

She became conscious of Tyler's eyes on her, and she looked up to smile at him, to assure him somehow that she was all right. She thought she owed him that much.

But when she looked up, she saw an enormous black form diving straight at the boat.

The sword formed in her hand, and she leaped to her feet.

Tyler's back was turned; he didn't see the creature diving right at him. Reese couldn't move fast enough either to intercept the diver or to warn Tyler; he caught sight of the sword in her hand and turned just fast enough to jump back and see the creature go straight through the bottom of the boat. It left a hole three feet across in the fiberglass, and water spouted and rushed up through it.

While Tyler scrambled to bail or find some way to repair the damage, Reese fixed her eyes on the water. The boat beneath her was unsteady footing, and she slipped and cracked her knee on a bench. The creature shot back out of the water at the same moment, blinding her with a combination of salt spray and darkness, but she had been expecting it, and she managed to stab straight despite her loss of footing and vision. She had it on the end of her sword, and it screamed out and flapped to get away. She held on tight and struggled to get back to her feet, though water was up to her knees. She drove the sword deeper.

With another scream, the creature died. She watched as the body transformed from huge and monstrous to the size of a gull, and then a gull's shape, colours, feathers. Her sword dissolved and the bird's body fell into the water.

The boat tipped, and Reese lost her footing and fell backwards into the water. Tyler was beside her, treading the waves. Her heavy shoes and socks pulling her down, she grabbed for the side of the boat—now just foundering in the water—and held on tight.

They were a full three miles from land.

"Can you swim it?" Tyler shouted.

Reese nodded, surprised at her own pluck. "If I get these boots off."

"Did something just try to kill us?"

"Yeah," Reese answered. "But it didn't succeed."

Tyler met her eyes. She couldn't read his. "Another renegade?"

She looked away.

"I'm not sure."

She was no longer convinced the first had been working alone.

* * * * *

Mary sat by her open window with her head in her hands, listening to the sounds of the village and the calls of birds overhead.

Rachel Starr Thomson

Where could April possibly be?

She and Richard had gone back out after they visited Diane Sawyer and spent most of the afternoon knocking on doors and asking questions. A few people had seen April run past yesterday morning—down the hill street toward the harbour. But nothing more. No one knew where she had gone or what had happened to her there.

Eventually Richard had ordered Mary back to the house to get some rest. He was still searching, of course. She knew him. He would never rest.

When a knock came on her own door, Mary stood slowly. Her feet moved themselves to answer it.

Chris Sawyer stood on the doorstep.

She regarded him for a second and then smiled. She opened the door. "Won't you come in?"

The broad-shouldered young man looked uncomfortable as he wiped his boots and removed his coat, but it was clear he was in no rush to leave. Mary put on a kettle and invited him to settle in the sparsely furnished sitting room. The house was one of the bigger homes in the village, even though it had only housed three of them for so long. There were several guestrooms habitually left empty, and the sitting room was large enough to hold ten or fifteen comfortably. A fireplace with a long brick mantle and step took up one end wall. Over it was a simple wooden cross, the only decoration on the walls. Long couches sat parallel each other on either side of the fireplace. The far end of the sitting room emptied into a hallway and stairs leading up to the bedrooms.

It was a house made for community, but it had not known

much of one for decades.

Mary handed Chris a cup of tea, which he handled awkwardly in his big hands. He looked so much like his father. Mary's heart warmed to him as it always did whenever she thought of the Sawyers, which was often. If only his mother wasn't so determined to keep the truth from her son.

But he was here now, and he was not a boy anymore—this was a man who sat on her couch, waiting for answers with quiet expectancy. Mary's mind was made up in an instant. She would give him answers.

As she maneuvered around the end of one long couch to take a seat across from Chris, regret struck her heart.

She should have done this a long time ago.

She sat down expecting to start the conversation and to spend most of it talking—giving the explanations he'd been waiting all his life for. He caught her off guard.

"There's something you need to know," he said.

Mary blinked.

"Mum told me about the Oneness," he said. "Two nights ago. Not everything—of course. But she told me about where it comes from, something of what it is . . . what you are."

Mary nodded in recognition.

"The reason she told me, after all these years, is there's a girl in our house. We rescued her—she jumped off a cliff. Tried to drown herself. Tyler caught her in a net and we pulled her in. She didn't tell us anything about herself, but then she . . ."

He hesitated.

"A demon attacked her and she killed it with a sword. Mum couldn't exactly pretend there was nothing unusual going on, so she had to explain to me some things about you people."

Mary frowned, confused. "You're saying there's a girl from the Oneness in your house? But—"

"She claims to be an exile," Chris said. "She says she's not part of the Oneness anymore. That scared Mum worse than I've seen anything scare her. All she would tell me is that the Oneness holds the world together and isn't supposed to break."

He set his tea cup down on the floor beside him and spread out his big hands in supplication. "Can you tell me more?"

Mary took a moment to respond, her mind working hard to catch up. An exile—that would explain the fear in Diane's eyes when Mary and Richard visited her earlier in the day—and her strange question about whether the Oneness ever cast out its own. The girl must be the Reese Diane had mentioned and then refused to say any more about. But Chris had to be mistaken. It wasn't possible for anyone to leave the Oneness—not without terribly wounding the whole. And if the girl could still draw sword against the demons, then she could not truly be separated from the body. Could she?

"I've never heard of . . . I don't think it's possible for anyone to be exiled," Mary said, aware that her response was lacking. But Chris was patient, leading the conversation to her continued surprise.

"She believes she is," Chris said. "I've never seen so much loss in anyone's eyes. Not even Tyler's when he lost his parents. She spent most of yesterday sleeping. I don't think she wants to be alive, let alone here with us." He cleared his throat. "Look,

I don't know why she's in my house, but I feel responsible for her. I want to help her. I figure you can teach me how."

"If April was here . . ." Mary stopped herself. He didn't know about April. She debated telling him. This all had to be interconnected somehow. She sighed and put down her own tea, clasping her hands and leaning forward.

"How much do you know about us?" she asked.

His answer could not have surprised her more if he had suddenly claimed to be the president.

"I know my mother is one of you," he said. "But I don't know why she won't admit it."

There were tears in Mary's eyes. She wasn't sure exactly how they had arisen. "That would be my fault," she said. "Diane doesn't want anything to do with us because of me. Because I . . ."

She stopped. This didn't have to be said now.

But no. The boy—this young man—deserved the truth. Hadn't she felt the regret of all the years just a few minutes ago? She should have told him long ago.

"Because your father died trying to help me," she finished, "and your mother has always held me responsible."

Chris was silent, staring at her in response. She looked away, uncomfortable under his gaze. She wondered what he saw—an enigma, a woman ageing who had once been beautiful, a servant who had tried to be faithful but brought more damage in her years than good. She cleared her throat. "I'm sorry."

"Thanks, I . . . appreciate that."

They both lapsed into silence again. Then he took up the

lead. Dogged and faithful like his father. "I don't know much else. I know you live among us but you aren't like the rest of us. Supernatural is the word. I know you're interconnected with each other somehow, and you see things, do things. Reese—the girl we rescued—told us that you fight demons and that angels serve you."

Mary raised her eyebrows. "In a manner of speaking."

"I also know you've been watching me my whole life," Chris said. "Watching over me, maybe I should say. Me and my mother both. She never acknowledges it, but she knows she owes you a debt."

"We don't abandon our own," Mary said.

"Which brings us back to Reese," said Chris. "Why is she exiled?"

Mary struggled with the question but tried to do it justice. "I don't know. I've never heard . . . exile is impossible, I think. Your mother won't recognize her connection with us, refuses to acknowledge it, and yet she is spirit of our spirit as much as you are bone of her bone. If something happened to her, we would all know it. What affects her affects us all. It's the way the Oneness works. For someone to be cast out—well, she must have done something."

"Something to separate herself?" Chris asked. "That doesn't make sense—you can't imagine the grief . . ."

"I think I can imagine it," Mary said. But would never want to. "No, something to cause the Oneness to reject her. Like . . . when a limb becomes so gangrenous it is a danger to the whole body, and amputation may be the only solution. The Oneness is a body. It's possible she may have done something so dark it introduced disease of some kind—something so dangerous to the whole that she had to be rejected."

She paused and picked up her tea cup again, needing the strong liquid to fortify her against the implications of all she was saying. "But I have never heard of it happening. Most of us would rather die all together than let one part be lost."

Lost. The word triggered something. An explosion went off in Mary's head and she saw, wreathed in shadows, April's face. She looked frightened.

"What's wrong?" Chris asked, standing, on alert. Mary tried to shake away the vision and come back to him. Most of us would rather die all together ... it was true. It was why Richard was still out searching and would never, ever stop.

"It's love that binds us together—love that's the blood in our veins," Mary said shakily. "We don't cast off our own!"

"What else is going on here?" Chris asked.

"We lost one of ours," Mary said. The words were bleak and terrible. "She disappeared yesterday morning. We don't know who took her or why ... but someone did."

He was silent a moment. Then, "Did you ask my mother for help? Sometimes she can see things."

Mary smiled wanly. "We tried. She told us she hadn't seen anything—we believe her. But she didn't tell us about Reese."

"You think they're connected?"

"They have to be."

Mary stood and wandered to the window, looking out to the road that plunged down into the village. The road April had run down and not come back. "The Oneness numbers in the millions. There are people like us all over this world, doing their part. But our cell is tiny. Only four of us . . . and one is your mother. The other two don't even know about her, or didn't until today. We get the occasional attack, the odd bit of trouble. Nothing like this."

Outside, the sun shone with deceptive brilliance and warmth. It was a beautiful day—as beautiful as the village had ever seen.

"When I came here, years ago, I was fleeing trouble. It followed, and that was the worst battle we've had—it took your father's life, and it hardened your mother's heart. After that things were calm. I was alone here, just me and your mother, for more than a decade. Then Richard came, and then April. This place was a haven for them too. But now . . ."

"Does this have something to do with Mum's dreams?"

Mary laughed bitterly. "Yes. Of course. Not that she shared them with us. But we've all been feeling it for months . . . a sense that darkness is closing in. That something is going to happen. That evil is coming."

Chris pondered the words for a few minutes and then said, with great conviction, "I don't think Reese is the evil. I mean, I understand what you're saying—that her being here means something is wrong. But I don't think she's evil. What you said about a limb being gangrenous . . . it makes sense. But it doesn't fit her. She's not diseased. She's just heartbroken."

Mary turned and regarded the young man. Handsome and confident and strong. It was like having Douglas back again.

"I think I'd better talk to Reese," she said.

He nodded, but after a long hesitation, and she knew he was considering it from the girl's point of view—trying to decide if it was wise, and safe, to allow the meeting. Every inch the protector. It struck her as incredible that Chris hadn't asked for more details about his father's death—and his involvement with the Oneness, and Mary, in general. He had to want to know. Diane had kept him in the dark all his life. But instead, his thoughts were for a girl he barely knew.

"You're a good man," she said softly.

"And what about your friend?" he asked. "The one who went missing? Are the police looking for her?"

"Richard is. We haven't called the police."

It was clear in his face that he disapproved.

"The police can't help when it's demons," she tried to explain. "And we think . . . well, all this trouble isn't human. Sometimes involving more people just makes things worse."

He was already heading for the door. "Come on, then," he said. "I'll take you to Reese."

He turned concerned brown eyes on Mary. "Just be careful. Please. She isn't whole."

The cottage was empty when Chris and Mary arrived. Chris did a preliminary search of the rooms and then returned to the tiny living room where Mary was waiting. "They're not here," he announced. "They must have gone out . . . probably fishing." He frowned. "I don't know if taking her out on the water was a good idea."

"She tried to drown herself two days ago?" Mary asked.

"Yes. I don't know what Tyler is thinking."

"Maybe he left without her?" Mary suggested. "She might have gone off on her own."

Chris paced, clearly agitated. "I don't like it." He stopped short. "I told you she was attacked here. In the side room—there's a big hole in the window to prove something bigger than a bat came through, even though that was all that was left of it after she killed it."

He looked at Mary as though to confirm that his words weren't crazy. She nodded.

"They possess," she said. "Demons don't have bodies of their own. They'll transform whatever they inhabit, but once they're driven out, the body goes back to its own form." She made a face. "Bats are a favourite."

"Do you want to see the room?" he asked. "Maybe there's something that could help you . . . some kind of clue."

She shook her head but stood anyway. "I don't think it will look different from any other attack." She let Chris lead the way through the kitchen and laundry room to the long side room with its musty carpet and old plaid couch. A wind outside was blowing clean air around the tarp. As she had expected, there was nothing in the room to indicate what had happened or why. They had disposed of the bat and cleaned up, and there was nothing to distinguish signs of the kill from any of the older stains on the shag carpet. But she closed her eyes and tried to put herself in the girl's shoes. An exile—separated from the Oneness, actually rejected and sent out. The very thought drove a weight into Mary's gut, and she cradled her arms across herself, trying to ease the bitterness of the thought. But the attack was strange. And that the girl had warded it off—with a sword she should not be able to wield outside the Oneness—that was stranger still.

Nothing about this situation was right.

"She said it was a renegade," Chris said.

"That's possible," Mary conceded. The demons would know if the girl had once been part of their enemy. They were spiteful enough to try to kill her for that. And yet, in light of all else that was going wrong, the attack didn't feel like a renegade.

It felt like a plan.

Rachel Starr Thomson

Suddenly the emptiness of the cottage took on an urgency. Whoever this girl was, whatever she meant, she shouldn't be out there alone. Mary turned on Chris. "Where did you say they might be?"

* * * * *

Once divested of their boots and coats, Reese and Tyler struck out for the nearest land—a tiny cove off the bay, shielded by the cliffs and some miles from town. The water was calm but the distance far, and when they had reached the warm sand, they lay panting and stretching their arms and legs for twenty minutes before either tried to speak. Despite her exhaustion, Reese kept herself on high alert, her eyes scanning the cliffs overhead for some sign of the enemy. They stretched away in sweeping lengths of red rock and scraggly pines and bushes, eventually capping beneath the blue sky. Deceptively idyllic.

Finally Tyler said, "No renegades?"

Reese cleared her throat twice. "No. I don't think so."

"Why are they targeting you?"

I wish I knew! her heart cried. Wasn't it enough that she had already lost everything that made life worth living? Wasn't it enough that her identity had been stripped, her love denied, her purpose eternally compromised? She was a wreck, a shell, a castaway destined to be undone by the elements. She was no threat to them anymore. So why attack her?

A tiny, desperate shred of hope stabbed her heart like shrapnel, and she denied it access.

That hope, unfulfilled, would destroy her completely.

The exile was not a mistake. It was real. There on the sand, she closed her eyes and let the pain wash over her full-force again, just to remind herself that there was no hope.

Why did she bother fighting back, anyway? They could come and kill her right now and she would welcome the freedom death brought.

Beside her, Tyler rolled onto his hands and knees and shook his shaggy head, damp curls spraying sand like a dog, and then stood and started brushing himself off in preparation for the long walk home.

This was why she bothered.

She turned her head and looked up at him. He was about her age, she decided, early twenties—maybe twenty-two, twenty-three. He was not Oneness. Yet he and Chris had risked things for her from the moment they pulled her out of the bay—from the moment they discovered her in the water, in a chance so improbable it could only be a freak accident or a carefully orchestrated plan. She had killed the first demon because it attacked in the cottage and would have gone on to harm her rescuers too. She had killed the second because it was diving straight at Tyler.

She sighed and squinted up into the blue sky. She was more alone than she had ever thought to be again, and yet in surrender or in fighting, she would be affecting other people. Somehow it didn't seem fair.

"Well," Tyler said, "we'd better get going. If we're lucky, Chris will have supper on by the time we get back."

Reese pulled herself slowly off the ground. Her clothes and hair were damp, and sand clung to every inch of her. She started brushing herself off as she thought over her options. It didn't take her long to resolve to go. This village was peaceful—storybook-like, really. If Diane Sawyer was anything to judge by, even the Oneness here was at peace. It wasn't fair to any of them for her to be among them, drawing the attention of the enemy. She needed to leave. She thought of trying to explain this to Chris, or even to say good-bye to him, and grew an unexpected ache in her throat. She would just go, then. Once they hit the streets, she'd say good-bye to Tyler and head out of town. He might try to follow her, but she knew how to keep herself hidden. It certainly wouldn't be the first time.

Thoughts of other days, other trips, other missions crept in around the edges of the walls she'd built to keep memories at bay. Other days when she'd found herself part of a tapestry unfolding, what most of the Oneness just called a plan. She wasn't sure how plans worked when you weren't part of the Oneness anymore, although others certainly had roles in them; but she was quite sure she didn't want her part, whatever it was, to unfold here. Better to get as far away as possible and hope to draw the whole tapestry after herself.

Tyler had already started trudging along the beach, and he called over his shoulder for her to follow. She did, planning ahead as she went. They were going to have to climb up into the base of the cliffs to avoid the incoming tide; the hike didn't look easy. It might be dusk by the time they were nearing the town, so it wouldn't be hard to slip away—perhaps even before they hit the streets. It was from a cliff height not far from here that she had jumped only two nights ago, but she barely remembered the paths she had taken then. She shivered a little as she pictured what might happen once she got away from Tyler and struck her own way into the cliffs—she would be vulnerable out there and not hard for the enemy to kill. An image of herself lying wounded or dead in the evening darkness made her shudder. For some reason death did not feel so welcome now.

* * * * *

April winced as she pulled her wrists against an outcrop of rock for the thirtieth time, pulling and sawing at the tape that had been wrapped in multiple layers around them. Her head had calmed to a raging but regular ache, and the pull against her hands and arms helped distract her from it. Besides, she was almost through.

The last bits of tape snapped through, and she wearily unwound the long strips and dropped them on the rocky floor. Having her hands free would do her no good as far as escape, but it went a long way toward making her more comfortable. Just in case, she wandered to the barred door, grabbed the grid, and shook it. The racket of iron against stone rattled painfully around her head and nearly turned her stomach, but it was secure. Miserably she returned to the spot on the floor where she could lean against a fairly smooth part of the rock wall, and she wondered how long she'd been here. And before that—how long had she been out? It seemed to her it was getting darker in the cave, indicating that it was getting late in the day. Whether it was the same day she'd been kidnapped or another one altogether she had no idea.

Suddenly realizing she'd been wearing a watch when she went out, she glanced down—it was gone. With a heavy sigh she leaned her head forward, resting it on her knees once again. She felt horribly weak, and for the first time she considered that she was hungry. She still had no idea why she was here, and she wondered if she would ever know. It would not be beyond the enemy to let her starve here . . . wherever "here" was. The thought almost made her smile. The enemy were cowards. More than one of the great saints, the Oneness who were most powerful and effective in the service of the Spirit, had been killed in these offhanded ways so that no one of the enemy would be found with blood on his hands. Maybe this prison had been used for the purpose before. April had no illusions about being a great saint, of course. She lived in a three-person cell in a tiny village overlooking the sea, and her work for the Spirit so far had consisted of little more than befriending lonely people and painting pictures.

Painting. An idea struck, attractive because it had the potential to distract her from hunger pains that were growing increasingly urgent. She got up and hunted around the cave until she found what she was looking for: a wet patch in the wall, streaked with mud. It was too dark by now to know whether the mud was red or not, but hoping, she dug her hand in and loaded it up with "paint," trekking across the cave to a wide wall. She stood in thought for a moment and then started a pattern she knew well: a rose vine, the same pattern that was tattooed across her shoulder. She swept a few long lines and then went back, working in the roses, and returned for more mud when she ran out, feeling her way for wet spots along the wall to make sure she was picking up in the right place.

How much time she spent on the mural she had no idea, but the supply of mud seemed endless. She stopped after she was content that she'd painted a full vine, beginning in one corner of the wall and arching up to the far corner, with offshoots and flowers and buds and thorns, and smiled to herself as she considered that the painting might not be visible at all come light—she had no guarantee that the mud would be coloured enough to show up. And it was quite possible that the painting was a disaster: she was working near blind, with a headache.

She sat down, feeling a little foolish but strangely happy all the same, and did her best to clean the last of the mud off her hands, using her track pants and the floor. Her hunger hadn't lessened, but she didn't feel quite as weak now. She was going to need to find a bathroom—most likely she'd have to designate a corner of the cave for the purpose, although the thought was depressing.

Her eyes were getting heavy, and although it briefly occurred to her that she might have a concussion and should avoid going to sleep, it also occurred to her that it might not matter if she did.

* * * * *

Tyler arrived back at the cottage shortly after the sun set. It had been a long, hard scramble up the cliffs to the town—probably not more than a five-mile trek, but it had taken well over four hours. Reese had been a trooper, never once complaining and keeping up a good pace, but they'd had to fight their way through thickets, scramble over a lot of steep rock, and backtrack more than once. When he finally saw the lights of the village winking in the dusk, Tyler felt like a burden had been lifted off his back, and he walked faster as he headed up the road to the cottage. Reese gave him a worn smile as he announced, "Almost home!"

Despite the steep grade of the road, Tyler picked up his pace. The lights were on in the cottage, and he could smell meat cooking. The smell was better than he would have expected from Chris, and he wondered if Diane had come over. He thought he glimpsed a female form passing in front of one of the windows, confirming the guess. It felt right that she should be there. He wasn't quite sure about the propriety of Reese staying with him and Chris alone, but somehow he knew Chris wouldn't want her to go stay with his mother. Troublingly, he was also fairly sure Diane wouldn't be open to Reese anyway. He didn't understand the dynamic between mother and son and guest. But, he realized, he cared about Reese, just like he cared about Chris and Diane.

He reached the front door and started to wipe his boots on the step, turning to say something to his travelling companion. Chris must have seen him coming, because the door opened before Tyler had been there a minute.

"Where's Reese?" Chris asked.

Tyler turned, the words "Right here" on his lips.

The words died away.

She was gone.

* * * * *

It was the light that woke April. Light that came softly from behind her like the glow from a lamp. She opened her eyes and smiled sleepily as the mural spread out before her in vivid red on pale rock: the vine and its roses in colour that seemed to pulse with life, branching, arching, looping across the cave wall.

Despite the darkness, she had hardly made a mistake.

Perhaps painting the cave wall wasn't such a childish thing to do after all.

Whether because she was so tired or because her head truly was injured, it took April a few minutes to wonder where the light was coming from. As she traced the contours of her painting she slowly became aware of someone sitting next to her. This didn't bother or frighten her at all—again, perhaps because she really did have a concussion. Maybe she was lapsing into a coma, she thought, and imagining the light.

Or maybe this was death.

She turned her head slightly, happy to find that for the first time since she'd awakened in the cave, movement didn't set her whole skull throbbing.

A woman she had never seen before was sitting next to her, and the light was emanating not from a lamp or from the dawn outside, but from the woman herself. The light was warm like flames in a hearth. The woman's eyes were fixed on the mural, and they sat together for some time, just taking it in.

"It's really fine work," the woman said eventually. "And important. You should keep at it, I think."

It was morning.

April was alone, and the cave was getting lighter—light enough that she could make out the lines of the mural, though not in the living relief she had seen it in last night. Her headache was still gone. The cave smelled, but the presence of the painting still made her happier, stronger.

Had she dreamed the woman?

Well, she wasn't dead ... so the visit hadn't been death. And unless she was dreaming now, she didn't think she was in a coma.

Ignoring the slight cramping in her stomach—too bad that hadn't gone with the headache—she got to her feet and headed for the wet mud in the back of the cave. "Keep at it," the woman had said.

It seemed to April like a fine idea.

This time she stood for a few minutes in front of the wall, the mud ready in her hands, considering. An image arose: one of the last she'd seen before all this. Bicycle tires whirling, a boy riding as fast as he could straight down the cobblestone street toward the bay. And then another image: the nets and crowded spaces of the fishing shack. And another: Nick's face. She hoped he was well, that the thugs had not had him in their sights in any way. She felt that he still needed her, and the frustration of being interrupted suddenly hit. So she began to sketch the images out in red paint, this time laying the mud down thickly and then scratching out a sketch with a thin bit of rock, using the light stone beneath to create the lines of the pictures. It would be a prayer, this painting. It was all that she could do here.

She became aware, as she worked, lost in concentration, that she wasn't alone. She could see no one, but her spirit sensed what her eyes could not. It was no great surprise.

She was Oneness, and she was never alone.

* * * * *

Chris had gone pale when Tyler arrived by himself, and he

rushed out into the gathering evening. Tyler, bewildered, had stumbled into the house to find that the visitor he had spotted was not Diane; it was a woman he didn't know, small and weathered, with dark hair silvered in strands and a face that was still powerfully attractive. She introduced herself as Mary and then stood peering around Tyler out the front door, clearly concerned about Chris.

When Chris came back twenty minutes later, having searched the immediate area as thoroughly as possible in the gloom, Tyler explained, "She was right behind me—we spoke when we got to the town. I have no idea when she left."

And Mary made both young men sit down and eat a dinner, which she had cooked, of ham and potatoes and cornbread. Tyler wolfed it down, starving despite himself; Chris ate as much as Tyler did but without apparently noticing it. Mary was remarkably unoffended by this.

"You are sure she left?" Mary asked Tyler once he had slowed down his eating somewhat. He was surprised at how much stronger eating made him feel. He hadn't realized just how harrowing the day had been. "She didn't get lost or . . ."

"She was right behind me," Tyler said. "It's a quiet night—I would have heard if something had happened to her. And we were practically at the base of the road when I talked to her last. She could see the cottage from where we were. She must have gone off alone on purpose."

Chris made an inarticulate sound. Tyler didn't bother to try to interpret it.

"One thing is certain," Mary said, "it's not an accident she came here. Two attacks in a row are not the work of renegades.

Something big is happening."

The story of the capsizing had come out in bits and pieces in between bites of dinner. Chris pushed his chair back from the table, the legs scraping across the kitchen floor. The room was so tiny that he shoved himself right up against the wall before he could even stretch his legs fully.

"So explain," he said. "You must have some idea what's happening."

Mary shook her head, frustration evident in the lines of her face. "If I could have talked to her, I might have learned something. As it is, all we have is a lot of disconnected pieces, and I can't make them fit. You said your mother has been dreaming ... well so have I. Dark dreams, prophetic ones. But they don't say anything clear. They're just foreboding. We've had letters from other cells, warning us that something is wrong, that they too can feel an attack pending. But that's all they say. We've all been sensing it. And now here we are: April's gone, demons are attacking ..."

Her voice trailed away. "I think Reese might be some kind of key. And now she's gone too."

"I think maybe she doesn't want to be a key," Tyler said.

The others looked at him.

"I mean, maybe she realized you were here waiting for her, and she didn't want to meet you. I've never seen anyone so broken in my life. She thinks you people rejected her, and that rejection is ... it's like death to her. I can see it. So maybe she's just scared to be around you."

"None of it makes sense," Mary mumbled.

She stood, pushing her own chair back into the wall. "At least we know she was here, and she went off on foot. I think it's time Richard and I went looking for her. He won't want to be pulled off searching for April, but maybe it doesn't have to be one or the other."

"I'll help," Chris said.

She gave him a long, searching look. "All right," she said finally. "And I'm going to get on the phone and see if any of the other cells of our acquaintance know anything about this exile of yours."

"The phone?" Tyler asked. "The Oneness uses the phone? I thought you were some kind of supernatural being."

Mary smiled. "We are. But we're not above a little old-fashioned sleuthing. Of course, if you really want to see more of the supernatural in action . . ."

"That's okay," Tyler said. The image of the thing that had capsized his boat and died at the end of Reese's sword was still fresh in his mind. "I don't mind old-fashioned." His mouth twisted downward. "I'll help too. I'm the one who lost her."

"Hey," Chris said. "I don't think it's your fault."

"Sure it is," Tyler said, his expression still grim. "I've been watching out for her all day. Don't know what I was thinking, taking my eyes off her at the end."

"You didn't know she was planning to run," Mary said.

He shrugged. "Maybe she didn't know that either, until she did it. She's grieving. People who are grieving might do anything."

Mary left the cottage with a heavy heart. The boys had decided to go back out and keep looking for Reese, searching the cliff paths with heavy-duty flashlights. She suspected they wouldn't find the girl. Despite Tyler's assertion that Reese's running off might have been unpremeditated, Mary doubted it. Those who were heavily afflicted with grief might be given to making unpredictable decisions, but they were not usually full of the courage, strength, or initiative it would take to go into the wilderness surrounding the village, in the dark, and face an active enemy.

Besides, whatever Reese was, Mary was quite sure she wasn't inexperienced. She had twice dispatched demons that struck at her without warning, and though Mary hadn't seen the fights, she knew that Reese had been fighting from a place of weakness and that the attacks had been fierce. And yet both times, there had been no question of who would win.

As Mary made her slow way down the cliff road to the village, the stars out overhead and glistening over the bay, she made a mental list of cells to call. They weren't directly connected to many anymore, but she should be able to find contacts for some of the larger ones. She planned to try the nearest cities first. Reese's level of expertise pointed to her being part of an active cell in a battleground, and that almost certainly meant an urban cell, not a rural one. Surely the right cell couldn't be that hard to find—the act of exiling would have rocked them to the core. Mary was surprised she hadn't heard rumours of it or received letters sounding the alarm. For that matter, she was surprised she hadn't felt the exile in her own soul. The Oneness was many, and some connections were much farther afield than others. Yet, something this drastic ought to affect everyone in a way that could be felt. The analogy she'd given Chris was not an exaggeration: an exile would be an amputation. Not like a death—deaths were not felt except by those who were closely connected to one another, because death did not break the Oneness. The body was one in heaven and on earth—and the distance between the two was not nearly so great as most people supposed.

She slowed around a bend in the road and prayed quietly, letting the Spirit in her speak. She felt the prayers humming in the air like vibrations on a string, creating music, creating a language not human and not bound by human limitations. She knew she was not alone in the prayers. The cloud—the family in heaven—prayed with her. Perhaps the angels did too.

Mary parked in the driveway and paused after stepping out of the car, letting her prayers swell higher and deeper. The moon was bright overhead.

When she stepped into the house, the vibration nearly knocked her off her feet.

Richard was home, and he had been praying.

To Mary's eyes the very walls of the house seemed washed in gold, and they quivered as with life. Richard was kneeling in the centre of the living room. Mary knelt beside him, and she felt her spirit expanding, stretching beyond her to the others, One in heaven and One on earth, One in Spirit and in truth. She closed her eyes, and time passed; how much she did not know. She felt eyes on her, the many eyes of the angels.

Finally Richard sighed.

He stood. Mary opened her eyes slowly and saw his hand outstretched. She took it and he pulled her to her feet, her knees and ankles protesting that she was getting too old for this.

"No sign of April," he said. "I looked everywhere. Knocked on nearly every door in town by one pretence or another. She's gone, Mary."

Gone, but not dead. As close as these three were—close like fingers on a hand—they would have felt her death. Yet Mary did feel something: a growing dread in the pit of her stomach. April was alive, and yet things were not well with her.

"April is not the only one we need to find," Mary said, sitting on the couch. Richard raised an eyebrow and sat down across from her. A clock in the kitchen ticked—it was nearing midnight. They'd been praying for hours. No wonder she felt so stiff.

"What is it?" he asked.

Mary explained about Reese. He did not interrupt, but when she finished, he said, "Is it possible? An exile? It can't be!"

"Even if it could," Mary said, "she doesn't act like an exile. The boys say she's torn apart with grief—dying of it. And yet the sword comes to hand when she's attacked, and she found the courage to go off alone tonight. They don't understand why, but I think she may be doing it for them. To draw the demons off. That's love, Richard. Whatever's happening to this girl, it isn't what it seems. I think if we find her, we might find the key to what's happened to April."

"One thing," Richard said. "About April. I spent time—a lot of time—in prayer today. If I wasn't knocking on doors, I was on my knees. And I think I saw some things in the spirit I haven't seen before. April's a lot . . ." he paused, trying to form the right words. "She's more than we thought. We thought the Spirit sent her here because she needed to heal and live at peace after that hell of a childhood. She thought she was assigned here just to help some lonely folks out."

"She's good at it."

"No doubt. But she's more than that. Her paintings, for one thing. I kept seeing them in the Spirit. They were opening windows and building bridges, and really changing things. She's been doing more, here, than we ever thought."

Mary spent a moment thinking about this. "Is that why . . ." she stopped. "It doesn't make sense for us to be targets. We aren't important enough. I assumed that whatever the Oneness has been feeling coming on, we were at the fringes of it. But you're saying April has been doing things, without anyone recognizing them, that make us important enough to draw fire. Serious fire."

"Exactly," Richard told her.

A pause. "Is that why she isn't dead?" Mary finally asked. "Because she's one of the great saints?"

"It's possible."

"Then she might be somewhere waiting to die."

The enemy did try to escape the justice of God that way, yes. Sometimes. Some individual part of the Oneness would become so powerful, so effective, that the enemy would come screeching out of the shadows to destroy that individual any way possible. Sometimes the results were bloody and quick. But the enemy had learned, over the years, that in the laws of the universe, of righteousness that was the character of God holding all things together, that such attacks would backfire. So in their ignorance and cruelty, they had long ago enacted a tradition of separating the great saint from the others and starving him, or her, or causing a death by the elements. Something that didn't actually leave blood on their hands.

But . . . April?

"We need to find her," Mary said.

* * * * *

When April woke again to see the woman sitting beside her, glowing with warm light as before, she concentrated not on the mural—which had grown and spread, all of the space on the left side of the vine filled with scenes and faces—but on the woman herself. She was not young but not old; perhaps in her late thirties or early forties. Her hair was dark and long, not styled like a modern woman's hair, and she wore a dress the colour of cream that was likewise simple and nondescript. Her skin had an olive glow, though perhaps that was just the effect of the light, and her eyes were dark. She smiled at April's examination.

"Who are you?" April asked.

"My name is Teresa," she said. April heard the faint trace of an accent in her voice, but she wasn't sure how to place it.

"You are Oneness," April said.

"Of course."

"From the cloud."

Teresa smiled again. "I am."

She stood and took a few steps closer to the mural, pouring her light over it. The light seemed to bring life to the painting, bringing out colours and textures April had not seen in the darkness. She marvelled at how her fingers had led her even in the murk of the day in the cave, using the contours and colours of the rock wall itself to add to the pictures she was painting.

Teresa reached out and touched one part of the new work, an unfinished sketch of the boy's face. April had finished the eyes, and they shone in the light as things alive.

"It's fine work," Teresa said. "It reminds me of my own, in some ways, but your attention to detail is better." She wrinkled her nose. "And your medium rougher."

April chuckled. "That is not exactly my fault."

In Teresa's presence, April realized, she was at peace in a way that seemed impossible given the circumstances. She had never met one of the cloud before, but the peace made sense; to own the perspective of heaven was to be perfectly at peace. Apparently the perspective was contagious.

Teresa turned and looked at her, and the expression in her eyes was unexpectedly solemn. "It can help you. Not only as paint, though you are doing well to use it that way—and I think you should continue. But in other ways."

April nodded weakly. It had been several days and nights—though she really didn't know what time it was—since she'd been taken. Or at least, that's what she thought.

Truthfully, she didn't know how long she'd been unconscious or how long she was sleeping between waking up. For all she really knew it had been just a day, or a week.

She'd had nothing to eat or drink, and she was beginning to feel the effects of dehydration. "Already thought of that," she said. "I sucked a handful earlier. Awful."

Teresa's smile was compassionate. "But important that you not give up. You know what they're trying to do to you—why they put you here. You should fight back."

"But why?" April asked. Suddenly she had tears in her eyes. She was tired. "If this is my time, why not just let it come? I'm not afraid to cross over."

"No, though the crossing over is not easy," Teresa said. "It was my time, when they did it to me. But I am not convinced it is yours."

April pushed herself up, sitting up against the wall and regarding her visitor more keenly than she had before. "They did this to you? Starved you to death?"

"Six hundred years ago," Teresa said. "But I still remember it."

"Why? What were you doing to them?"

Teresa waved her hand at the mural. "Painting. And rescuing children. In my day, in the countryside many children were dying of plague or abandonment. I and others of the Oneness, sisters who came to my side, brought as many as we could into the abbey we shared. We mothered more than two hundred of them. And many became Oneness, and threats to the enemy. There was one we rescued—"

Teresa's eyes grew distant as though she could see the child's face. She came back to the present and lightly brushed her fingers across the sketch of the boy. "A boy like this one. He would grow to be a mighty warrior against the darkness, and I was his trainer, his friend and strength. The paintings were teaching him things and giving him strength. So the enemy chose to take me out of the way."

"And you were never rescued," April said.

"No. It was my time."

"Starving can't be easy."

"It is not. But when I had crossed over, I lived to see the designs of the enemy turned back upon themselves a thousand-fold. They think to escape vengeance through their machinations, but they are fools and blinded by their own deceptions."

"Are you one of the great saints?" April asked.

Teresa smiled as she thought over the question. "They call me that," she said. "But on this side, greatness looks different."

"That's the one thing I don't understand," April said. She found that words were hard to get out—her hunger and thirst were taking a greater toll on her than she realized. "I'm not anything they should be afraid to kill."

"We don't know who we are," Teresa said. "None of us know who we are until we cross over, and even then, much is mystery. I didn't. You don't."

April considered this. "Why are you here?" she asked.

"For companionship," Teresa said. "I do not think you are going to die. But you will—you are already—experiencing a little of dying. At such times, it is good not to be alone."

* * * * *

Reese followed the cliff paths for hours that night, not sleeping. The lack of sun made her still-damp clothes grow colder and clammier, and by the time the sun rose, she was sore, shivering, and bruised from stumbling and tripping through the dark. Somehow her feet remembered the way. She caught sight of the blacktop highway in the early morning light and gladly dragged herself out to the side of the road, raising a thumb and finding that she was too tired to care about how stupid it was to hitchhike alone.

So alone.

There was little traffic on the road. Those cars that did pass ignored her. Too tired to hold memories or thoughts at bay, she swam in the misery of the last week and all it had meant—drowned in the pain of alienation. The scenes played themselves out over and over again. The words spoken, the growing gulf between her heart and those of her companions, her actions that she couldn't take back, their actions that she couldn't forget. Stab after stab after boot after weight dragging her, pulling her down.

It wasn't supposed to happen like this. Oneness was never, ever supposed to turn on itself.

A battered Ford station wagon passed, slower than some of the other vehicles, and Reese leaned forward, making herself more visible, hoping to inspire compassion. The car kept going.

When it had first started happening, she had told herself they were all just tired, weary from a mission that was frustratingly hard. She just had to forgive it, and she needed them to forgive her.

She dashed tears away with the back of her eyes. No one was going to pick her up if she stood there crying like a fool.

They'd said it was her fault. If she hadn't held so doggedly to her course, if she'd listened to them, if she had been willing to be wrong. They were right. They had to be right—otherwise the Spirit would not have allowed this. And yet, looking back, she did not know what other course she could have taken. She'd followed the voice she believed was the voice of Oneness, the voice of the Spirit, believing she was the one with ears to hear and the others should follow, as they had always followed, as they had always acted as one even when some could not see, or hear, or understand. She'd believed they would act in trust. In faith. As Oneness always did.

There had been twelve of them, all from the city cell in Lincoln where Reese had been trained and spent most of her life. They had been sent out together on a mission to break up a hive, a grouping wherein the demonic had become centralized and taken control of human beings in a mocking facsimile of unity. But the hive was bigger and more dangerous than they'd realized going in, and they were fighting in the dark on so many levels. Then finally Reese had heard. She was a thousand times sure she had heard: she knew what to do, how to attack to break the hive's power. Where to find the demonic core that powered it. She had told the others, but many hesitated. They thought she was wrong. She asked them for trust. They started going out together, making small forays, attacking according to Reese's lead. It didn't seem to have any effect, but she was sure this was the right way to go. The results would come if they were just faithful.

One night she took two of the others, and they went out and made an attack that became a bloody, vicious battle. An ambush. One of the three crossed over. Reese knelt by his side, clutching his hand, saying the words of crossing as his soul left his body. She swore fealty and revenge while their third companion still fought. Then Reese took up her sword and together, the two vanquished their foe. They believed they had broken the power of the hive in doing so.

And when they came home, flushed with victory and aching from the fight, it was only to be denounced. The Oneness declared she had been wrong. She had wasted the life of one of their own for no reason but selfish ambition. They condemned her together, as One.

The ties had cut. Exile. The Spirit gone, with everyone who was part of it, like she'd experienced a hundred million deaths of all she held dear, consciously and unconsciously, all in a single moment.

She wasn't sure when her legs had given way, when she had ended up kneeling on the side of the highway with gravel digging into her knees and sobs wracking her body and soul. The thought came. You are never going to be picked up like this.

And just as it did, she heard tires on the blacktop and saw lights and then a car pulled over. An old man was driving, white-haired and concerned.

"Are you all right?" he asked. "Come, get in."

I'm not all right, her heart answered back. I will never be all right again. But all she said was, "Thank you."

She pulled her broken self off the shoulder and into the car and closed the door behind her.

* * * * *

At the top of the cliffs looking down over the bay and the village, a man stood.

His face was bloodied and swollen. His leather jacket and jeans were torn and likewise streaked with blood—his own, mostly. He held a sword in his hand.

Here? he asked.

No, a voice answered. She's gone. She left.

Then why am I here?

Because she needs to know the truth.

I still don't understand . . .

There is a mouth here that will give it to her. You need to find that one and give him the words to say.

The man nodded. He was a big man, broad-shouldered, powerful. Blond hair was tied back in a ponytail. His eyes scanned the village, looking for the others. They were there—a man, on his knees, rending the heavens with his prayers.

That one?

No.

But that one would be a worthy ally nonetheless. He kept looking. He saw the small woman who had headed the cell here for many years. She looked grieved and weary. And he saw more. Two others. Neither where he expected them to be, or doing what he expected them to be doing.

As he looked down the path, a form took shape. A dark-haired woman with olive skin and a beautiful face.

"Greetings, brother," she said.

He bowed in respect. This woman was no small saint.

"My lady," he said.

She smiled. "You have grown courtly in your passage. Does anyone in your time use a greeting like that?"

"We pick things up here and there," he said. "Books, television."

"Do you understand what you have to do?"

"I think I do. But it doesn't make sense to me."

"Why should today be any different? The plans never make sense to us. That is why they require faith. Surely you should know that."

"If I may ask, my lady, why are you here?"

"I have a mission of my own," Teresa told him. "But I wished to encourage you in yours."

He marvelled as he looked down at the village again. "Such a small place," he said. "A tiny cell. Who would have dreamt so much consequence would be attached to it?"

"We do not know what we are," Teresa said. "Nor of how much consequence. The view is different from this side, but even we in the cloud do not see the whole. As you know now."

She laid a hand on his shoulder, not put off by the blood and the dirt and his battle-weary aspect.

"Go, friend," she said, and spoke the benediction of Oneness for ages past: "You are not alone."

At first, Tyler thought he was imagining the man who stood in his path. It was dark, for one thing, an hour yet before dawn, and he could see the man too clearly, almost as though he exuded some kind of light. His search for Reese had taken him up into the cliffs again. Chris was searching on a lower path, a hundred feet down. This stretch of path was narrow and rocky and beset before and behind with prickly scrub; it was not exactly an auspicious place to meet an angel.

Which was Tyler's second guess. Because the man was still there, stern and tall and muscular, and now that he looked more clearly, the man was glowing, or something like it—at least it wasn't moonlight that made him so clear against the dark cliffside, and it certainly wasn't Tyler's flashlight.

He clicked that off. The man was still lit.

"Umm," Tyler said. "Are you an angel?"

The man ignored the question and asked one of his own instead. "You're Tyler MacKenzie?"

"I'm not sure I should answer that question," Tyler said.

"I have a message for you."

Ignored again. Tyler cleared his throat. "For . . .?"

"For Reese," the man said. "Listen to me. When you find her, tell her that she's wrong. Tell her Patrick says she's wrong. Things are not what they look like. Tell her I know it's dark, but this is the darkness that requires patience."

"You're Patrick?" Tyler asked.

"Yes."

"And you're an . . . angel?"

Patrick shook his head. The longer he stood there, the more human he looked. In fact, Tyler thought he could see dirt and scratches on the man's skin. And he was wearing a leather jacket.

"What are you?" Tyler pressed.

"I'm . . . dead. But not how you think of death."

"Apparently not," Tyler managed. Suddenly his questions were almost more than he could manage, and he felt a sudden fear that the man would disappear and leave him there with everything he wanted to know unanswered. "Wait, you said Reese is wrong. About the Oneness? She's not really an exile?"

"Just tell her what I said, all right?" The dead man looked uncomfortable at this whole situation, a fact which Tyler found ironic.

"Do you know where she is?" Tyler took a step forward.

"No."

"Why don't you go find her yourself? Why am I the messenger?"

The man shook his head, apparently as frustrated as Tyler felt. "I don't know, okay? None of this is normal."

"You're telling me," Tyler said under his breath.

The man heard, and to Tyler's surprise, he laughed. "We're even, I guess. Listen, I don't know where Reese is. Just that you will find her—I'm sure you will. If you weren't going to find her, I wouldn't have been given a message to pass on through you."

Tyler considered this, but other questions were pressing hard and fast on him. "Can you tell me how you're here? I mean ...you said that you're dead ..."

"I am," the man, Patrick, answered. "But death is a bit flexible when you're Oneness."

"Why?"

"We are risen." Patrick fixed his blue eyes on Tyler. "Listen, kid, I don't know the plan ...I mean, I don't know exactly what's going on here. I was told to give you a message, and you would give the message to Reese. But if you want some advice—and you should—don't let your role end there."

"What do you mean?" Tyler asked, feeling all at once dwarfed by the night sky and the bay and the way that death wasn't death, but was standing and talking to him like a brother. Or a father.

"The Spirit isn't wasteful," Patrick went on, "so me talking to you ... most likely it's for you too. I can see you got questions, a lotta them. And some hurts too, if I'm not imagining it. Well, listen: there are answers. You might just have to go looking for 'em. But the fact that I'm standing here, talking to you, means they're already looking for you too."

Tyler swallowed a lump in his throat. "I'm not sure what to do with that."

"Nobody ever is. You'll figure it out. Just do what comes to hand. And let yourself believe in things."

Tyler cracked a smile. "Like dead people talking to me?"

"Things like that. Although the power of visitations from beyond the grave is generally overstated. Ask Reese, when you find her."

"Right. Any clue how I'm supposed to do that?"

Chris's voice carried up from below, shouting Tyler's name. He tore his eyes from Patrick for a moment and caught the sweep of Chris's flashlight on the path below. He waved. "Up here!" When he looked back at the man in the pathway, Patrick's eyes glinted.

"I don't know where she is. But just a thought. It ain't like Reese to run from a fight. She'll run to it more often. You want to find Reese? Find the fight."

Chris's footsteps were pounding the dirt of the path. Tyler opened his mouth to ask another question, but Patrick vanished.

The path was plunged into darkness.

A moment later, the beam of Chris's flashlight shone from behind.

"Your battery go dead?" Chris called.

Tyler switched his own light back on and turned to face his approaching friend. "No. Just trying to use the natural light . . . see if I can see anything."

Chris shielded his eyes as Tyler's ray caught him in the face.

"Not much of that tonight."

Tyler lowered his light. "Sorry. When you were below, did you . . . did you see anything up here?"

"No," Chris said. "Your light went out and I wanted to make sure you were all right."

Tyler turned back and stared at the place in the path where Patrick had stood. "I hope I am. Do you believe in ghosts?"

"I don't know. I believe in things . . . that there are a lot of things in this world we don't know much about, and lots of things people have been hiding. Ghosts might figure in there somewhere. Did you see one?"

Tyler kept staring at the path. There was no sign that anyone had been there, but then, it was so dark he might not see such a sign if it was there. "I may have."

"It talk to you?"

Tyler nodded. "Said he had a message for Reese."

Chris stood a little straighter at this. "He say where to find her?"

"He said go where the fight is."

Chris shone his flashlight beam in a broad arc, cutting a trail of light through the dark air beyond the cliff toward the bay. The moon had gone behind clouds; the water was barely visible, highlighted only by the lights of the village. "Seems like we're in the wrong place, then."

Tyler nodded, and by unspoken agreement, both headed back toward the trail that would take them home. As far as they knew, Mary was still there—doing what they weren't sure.

Praying, maybe. Having visions or dreams that might help them. They had felt out of their element from the start, going into the night like this. Nothing that was going on was really human; how could a search in the scrub and the dark really help anything? But they'd had to do something. They both knew that.

* * * * *

Mary sat on the phone in Chris's kitchen and let it ring for what seemed like twenty minutes before someone on the other side finally picked up. It was a voice she hadn't heard in decades, and they exchanged greetings and pleasantries for a few minutes before she sat back in the chair at the kitchen counter and braced herself to start digging.

"David, tell me, do you know a girl called Reese?"

She forced her voice to remain calm, nonchalant, though inside her soul was in turmoil. This was not the first call she had made. She'd been making others all through the night, calling up cells she knew better, people whose hearts were linked to hers by an unbreakable chain. This cell, the Lincoln cell, she did not know nearly as well. For some reason she had dreaded calling them.

Perhaps that should have told her everything she needed to know.

David was silent on the other end. She wondered what he looked like now, twenty years after she'd met him as a young man—just before the greatest tragedy of her life. He had been new to the Oneness, she a member from childhood. Both had become leaders since then.

His silence made her want to jump out of her skin.

Finally he said, in a voice heavy, "Yes, we know Reese."

Mary licked her lips. Stay calm. "She came from your cell?"

"Listen, Mary, what do you know about this girl?"

"Not as much as I'd like. She passed through the village but I was never able to come into contact with her."

"Be just as glad you didn't," he said. His voice was sharp. "She's dangerous. Mary . . . she's been exiled."

"Yes." Her voice was small—so small, and scared. She hated the sound of it. "I know that."

"I know you don't understand." His voice was strained, but he was trying to reassure her; she could hear that caring, protective timbre in it despite the weariness. "I don't understand myself. We're still trying to figure out what happened. How she turned against us like that."

Mary cleared her throat. "Can you tell me about it?"

"She betrayed us," David said. "I don't know what happened to her . . . how the enemy got to her. But he did. She was working against us—lying, poisoning the body. She was on a mission to attack a hive, but they somehow got control of her. She led one man to his death." David sounded like he was trying not to cry. "A good man. Patrick. A brother to me. Reese led him straight into a trap and stood by while he was slaughtered. She tried to come back, but we could smell it—see it—all over her."

"Like disease," Mary said. Her voice was still so small.

"Like gangrene." He paused. "We had to do it."

"I didn't know it was possible."

"Neither did I. But a man can't imagine sawing his own leg off until that leg is killing him. Then he finds strength he didn't know he had."

They talked a few minutes more. When Mary hung up the phone, she sat beside it woodenly, staring into the tiny living room, weighed down.

The front door opened, ushering in two exhausted young men and the light of dawn. They didn't look surprised to see her. They did look like they needed sleep.

Chris strode across the living room and placed both palms on the kitchen counter, leaning over toward Mary.

"Tell me," he said in a voice raspy with weariness and the outdoor air, "if we wanted to find the heart of whatever's going on—the fight, if you want to put it that way—where would it be?"

Mary didn't expect the words that tumbled out of her own mouth. "You're not equipped for this."

Chris banged a hand on the counter, and Mary jumped. "What is that supposed to mean?"

"This is a supernatural battle," she said, leaning forward herself, gathering fire. "You can't fight it. You shouldn't even be in the middle of it."

"Well, it seems we are," Chris said. His voice sounded bitter. "You told us about angels and demons. What about ghosts?"

"Ghosts?"

"Dead people! Dead people walking around and talking to guys like Tyler in the middle of the night." Chris pointed to his friend, who was still standing in the doorway as though he wasn't sure what to do next.

"You saw . . ."

"His name was Patrick."

Tyler's words fell into the room like snow, and Mary was suddenly, instantly, fully awake. Her eyes passed Chris and focused on the younger boy.

"What did he tell you?"

"He said to tell Reese that she's wrong and nothing is what it looks like. She's not an exile . . . she's wrong."

Mary abruptly turned her eyes back to Chris. "You want to know where the battle is?"

"Yeah."

"I think I might know. It's in Lincoln." She set her jaw grimly. "It's in a hive."

* * * * *

Although the cave was pitch-black at night and somewhat dim during the day, April was losing the ability to tell the difference. Between her hunger and the adjustment of her eyes to the darkness, nothing really looked normal. The cave stank, and she could feel her body breaking down; she was dizzy and faint, and it was getting harder to think straight. It seemed to her that the breakdown was moving too fast to be due just to lack of food. Shouldn't people be able to fast for a while without suffering too terribly much? A week at least? She was still getting water from the mud, and needing it badly enough that she almost didn't mind how nasty the whole experience was.

She suspected her head injury was at least partially the culprit for how bad she felt.

But all that paled in comparison to her painting. Whenever she was awake, she crawled or staggered or walked to the mud and covered her hands with paint. Even in the darkness she could see her work now, clear as daylight before her eyes, and she was driven to it: driven by it, driven through it. The mural had sprawled. It now covered not only the original wall, but two others, and parts of the ceiling that were low enough for her to reach. The rose vine grew through all of it, bearing flowers and leaves and thorns. All around it were people and places, connected by the vine. Nick. The old people at the home she used to go and visit. Various fishermen and the woman who ran the bar and would sometimes give April a coffee and talk to her. Mary. Richard. Even Teresa. And others—people she didn't know, people she'd never seen before.

At some point the pictures stopped being just pictures and started telling a story. Where the story came from she was not sure. She felt that she was getting it from the Spirit. It surprised and dismayed her even as it sometimes gave her hope. Other creatures joined the plot—angels and demons, gods and demi-gods, intersecting with the vine and warring one with another. It was a fantastic panoply, a myth spreading itself within this hidden dying place for no eyes but hers—and those of the already dead—and she did not know why but she knew that it had to be done. While she worked on it, her hunger and thirst dimmed and her eyes cleared. She was often aware of Teresa's presence lingering in the cave, though not often visibly. When she did come visibly, April noticed a gauntness to her form, a hollowness to her cheeks, that spoke of her own difficult history.

Someday, the Oneness believed, those who had passed into the cloud would receive their own bodies back again, fully healed and restored and made new. But their spirits, for now, bore some of the marks of their past history on earth.

April often wondered about Teresa and wished they might spend more time talking face-to-face, as friends. But though the cloud was always close, and though the Oneness held, that a separation did exist between them was evident. Thankfully, that did not stop Teresa from coming and looking over the painting, commenting on it now and then. Always she told April that it was important, this thing she was doing. That the story needed to be painted here in the dark. And she reiterated, once or twice, that she did not think April was meant to die here.

Well, April reflected as she lay on the floor of the cavern after a long painting spell, letting the rock overhead meld into the familiar fuzzy darkness that was part absence of light and part April's own weariness, no one in the cloud was infallible.

A deeper darkness was pressing in. She could feel it—a pressure gathering around her head, around her heart. Feebly, she fought it—Teresa had told her many times to fight it. But she was so tired.

April closed her eyes.

Seated at April's side, Teresa bowed her head and said a prayer for her friend.

The roar of passing semitrucks on the highway dulled Reese's discomfort as she rode in silence beside the kindly old man who had picked her up. Awkward but trying his best to be helpful, he tried to make conversation once or twice before giving up and contenting himself with driving. After that the trucks and the miles took over, and neither felt a need to talk.

It was an hour's drive into Lincoln, and to her surprise he took her all the way. He dropped her off next to a corner store and stuffed a few dollars into her hand. Genuinely grateful, she thanked him.

"It was nothing," he said, and drove off. Untrue, she thought. Kindness is always something. His unassuming help made her think of Tyler and Chris, and she pushed away a sense of guilt for leaving them. She had done it for them, after all. The enemy was after her. Better that she die here, in a city so full of people that everyone was anonymous, in an alley or a parking lot somewhere, than that the final fight happen in the village where its repercussions would touch everyone.

Exile she might be, but Reese had never stopped thinking in terms of connection. All things were connected, after all, though few recognized or believed it. The Oneness was different because they recognized and threw themselves into the connection. For that reason they functioned as the threads holding together a world that was trying to break itself apart.

The door buzzed as Reese pushed her way into the corner store. She stood at the counter in the back of the store for a moment, the floor beneath her scuffed and dirty from those who had come before her. Her eyes roved over the line of coffee thermoses, paper cups in three different sizes, and a sausage warmer next to a basket of half-warmed pastries. Quickly counting out the money in her hand, she grabbed a plastic-wrapped danish and a large coffee. The clerk barely acknowledged her as he took her money and made scant change.

Back outside, Reese looked over the street and considered where to go. The Lincoln skyline—nothing impressive, just a few central banks, law firms, and other businesses in three midsize skyscrapers—loomed to the west, probably a twenty-minute walk away. On the other hand, she could stay out here in the grungier, less professional part of town, with its gas stations and restaurants and corner stores crowding the main streets and housing divisions at the back of them.

Or she could go to the warehouse.

The thought struck her with cold force. She looked down at her hand, picturing the sword forming there. Why not? She was going to die anyway—and if it came down to it, she wanted to. So why not wade back into the thick of the hive's power and take out as many of the enemy as she could?

Why not do one last thing for the Oneness, even if they

didn't want her help anymore?

She would be going alone. No one else to get hurt. And no need to stand around on street corners and wait for an attack.

But what if she couldn't access the sword? What if that last vestige of Oneness had worn off? She wasn't sure why it had stayed in the first place. Chances were good she would find herself in the midst of a demonic swarm unarmed.

You're going to die either way, she reminded herself. Six of one.

She flexed her hand and remembered when she had clutched Patrick's while he died. He had gripped so tightly, and she had vowed to avenge him.

Well, she would keep the vow.

Resolute, she started down the street. She'd had the man drop her off in an unideal part of town—it would take her forty minutes to get to the industrial quarter where the warehouse was. That was okay. She'd have time to plan.

* * * * *

As they barrelled down the highway in Chris's truck, Tyler kept casting glances at the tall black man who shared the back bench with him. Something about Richard's presence staggered him. It was like the man carried the aura of some other world on his shoulders. Every time Tyler got near him, he felt like was brushing up against the universe.

Mary's earlier words bothered him more the closer they got to Lincoln. This is a supernatural battle. You can't fight it.

It was true, wasn't it? He and Chris weren't equipped for this. He'd seen demons twice now, both attacking without warning, and if Reese hadn't been so quick—and armed—he might be at the bottom of the bay at this moment. Richard and Mary didn't look like they were carrying swords, but they possessed something—some kind of power—nevertheless. He could feel it. Especially on the man.

Richard looked over and caught Tyler staring. Tyler jerked his head away, but he didn't miss Richard's smile. "You have something you want to ask me?"

A semi on the left honked as Chris pulled in front of it, dodging heavier traffic coming up on the right.

"I was just wondering about you," Tyler said honestly. "And about how to fight this . . . whatever we're going to fight."

"We hope you won't have to," Richard said. "But what were you wondering about me?"

"You have a . . . an aura. Something." Tyler shifted uncomfortably. "I don't know what I'm trying to say."

"I think I do." Richard's eyes were kind. "You're feeling the power of prayer."

"Prayer? Like 'Now I lay me down to sleep'?"

Richard laughed. "Not exactly like that. Prayer is much more than recitation. It's participation. It opens up pathways between heaven and earth and brings power down by lifting weakness up."

"That doesn't make a lot of sense to me."

"But it's what you're feeling."

Tyler gave it some thought. "So you're like this because why?

You're not praying right now."

Richard thought out the question before answering it. "Prayer can be continuous, without ceasing," he said. "It's a discipline of keeping your heart fixed. I try to do that. So right now I am praying, in a way. But I'm also talking to you, so my focus is elsewhere, yes. I'm 'like this,' as you put it, because I'm prayed up, as some folks would put it. I've been praying and fasting since April disappeared."

"Wait, that was days ago," Tyler said, sitting up a little straighter. "You haven't eaten since then?"

"No."

"But all this praying and fasting didn't help you find her," Tyler pointed out. "You still don't know where she is. And now you're not even looking—you're chasing down Reese."

Richard looked troubled. "I hope Reese will lead us to April. You're right, I haven't found her."

"But why not? With this supernatural access of yours . . ."

"It's not a vending machine," Richard said. "Put something in and get whatever you ask for out, just like that. Sometimes you don't even know what you're asking for. And it's not a game of odds—just keep trying and eventually you'll get lucky. It's participation, remember. I don't pray to get around the plan; I pray to be part of it."

"The plan?" Tyler asked.

Mary spoke this time. She'd been following the conversation from the seat beside Chris. "The world is unfolding according to design. Think of a tapestry with different threads connecting just as they are meant to. We call those threads plans. They are directed—they have purpose. But we are in the tapestry, so we can't see where every thread leads until we get there." She reflected. "Sometimes not even then."

"So all this . . . Reese getting her heart broken, and your friend being kidnapped or killed, and demon attacks, all that . . . this is all some plan?"

"I know it's hard to understand," Richard said. "But we aren't alone in this world. We all make choices, take actions, do things—for ourselves, to one another. We make up the fibres in the tapestry, and every one is truly significant. But another hand guides every fibre into threads and the threads into a picture, a plan. Nothing is disconnected, and nothing is outside the Spirit."

"Not even us?"

The question came from Chris, who despite driving aggressively, almost angrily, was following the conversation. His question was carefully controlled.

"Mary said we couldn't fight this battle because we aren't supernatural," Chris pointed out. "Because we aren't like you. But you're telling me we're part of this plan business too? That we're in the Spirit somehow just like you are?"

"Yes," Richard answered. "Nothing that exists exists outside the Spirit. The difference between us is not that. The difference is that we are not only inside the Spirit, but the Spirit is inside us. And that is not true of you."

The words sounded harsh, yet Tyler believed them fully. He could feel the difference. He was not what Richard was. A thousand "Now I lay me down to sleeps" would never call down the kind of power that was swirling around Richard like dust motes in light. And he could feel other things too. He and Chris were close, like brothers, but they weren't like Mary and Richard. In some invisible way Tyler could not see but only feel, he knew they were truly One. He wouldn't have been surprised to discover that their hearts were beating in sync.

"How do you change?" Chris asked. "What makes somebody Oneness? Or were you just all born like this?"

"Not at first," Mary said. "You become Oneness when you are born a second time—born of the Spirit."

"So how do you do that?"

Richard smiled gently. "That is a mystery. No one really knows."

Tyler eyed Chris nervously. His friend was more pent up than Tyler had ever seen him. For some reason these people mattered to Chris in a way that they didn't to Tyler, even though he was the one who had seen demons and ghosts and talked to Reese at length. These people with their non-answers might make Chris explode.

To Tyler's surprise, Chris was silent. He swerved into the passing lane again, speeding past a convoy of dump trucks, and then pulled back into the right. A sign declared it was only twenty miles to Lincoln.

"How did it happen to my mother?" he asked, finally.

Tyler bit his tongue in shock. Diane was Oneness?

It made . . . sense. But she wasn't quite like these other two. His mind raced. She had never claimed to be Oneness. She was intuitive and spiritual in a way others weren't, but she wasn't eager to claim it and never seemed happy when she shared things she knew. Was that why she was so different from these two? Because she didn't want to be what they had embraced?

"The same way it happens to any of us," Mary said. "She looked into the truth and was born of it."

Tyler sighed heavily. "You people aren't real helpful."

Richard shrugged apologetically. "There isn't a good way to explain it. You will know when the Spirit is seeking you. At some point you yield—or you don't. The moment of yielding is the moment of birth."

"And then what?"

"And then you are alive. Forever."

The words brought Patrick to mind. What had he said? We are risen.

"What is it like to be one of you?" Tyler asked.

Mary answered, "It's hard. But we would never trade it."

"My mother would," Chris said. His voice was hard again.

"We don't know why your mother is the way she is," Richard started, but Mary gave him a look, and he stopped. "To be honest, I didn't know about your mother," Richard finished. "Not until we went to her to ask for help finding April."

"Help that she wouldn't give you."

"I don't think she had anything to offer us, or she would have," Mary said. "Your mother tries to stay out of conscious participation in the plans as much as she can. But she doesn't work against us."

Tyler raised an eyebrow and waited for more explanation, but none came. He sensed that Mary and Chris both understood this dynamic better than he or even Richard. At least this explained why Chris seemed so tense. It wasn't just that he was worried about Reese. This was personal.

The exit loomed up under an overhang on the right, and Chris pulled off the freeway, following Mary's hastily given directions. The truck bounced through a pothole as it pulled onto a city street in a dingy, grass-through-the-sidewalks neighbourhood. "Are you sure this is the right place?" Tyler asked. For some reason he'd expected the Oneness to be headquartered somewhere more impressive.

"This is it," Mary said. She smiled at him like she knew what he was thinking. "Never judge a book by its cover."

Tyler shrugged, uncomfortable, and Mary told Chris to take a left at the light. They drove past a corner grocery store with its windows plastered with flyers and took a few more potholes on their way to the end of the street. Two blocks down they pulled up in front of a two-story vinyl-sided house with a front porch covered in vines. The house was big for the lot; strips of grass on each side were all that constituted a yard. The asphalt driveway was crammed with four cars; other cars lined the street on either side, belonging to who-knew-what homes. Although the house looked old, it and the yard belonging to it were neat and clean—less rundown, overall, than any of the surrounding homes.

Chris found a place to park a few houses down, and all four piled out of the truck. Richard cleared his throat. "Well, we're here."

With a nod to Mary, Richard took the lead. Chris and Tyler fell in behind them, Tyler feeling particularly conspicuous. Could anyone in this distinctly city neighbourhood tell how much he and Chris didn't belong here? They were fishermen and village boys through and through. Thank God.

As they turned up the crowded driveway to the front door, Richard paused, looked over at Mary again, and then addressed the boys. "I think it's best if you don't mention Reese," he said. "Perhaps not Patrick either. In fact, maybe you'd better let Mary and I do all the talking."

"Fine with us," Chris said, and Tyler nodded. He wasn't sure what in the world he would say to these people anyway.

Richard rang the bell, and the foursome stood back to wait for someone to come to the door. It was while they waited that Tyler became aware of a sensation in the air—something much like what he had felt sitting next to Richard, but not quite so expansive. It was like something was present and active in the atmosphere all around them, but whatever it was could not be seen or heard, only felt. He glanced at Chris but couldn't tell what his friend was feeling or thinking.

Tyler narrowed his eyes and focused on the front door. The Oneness was unnerving. He wasn't sure he liked this introduction into their world—or the fact that it seemed his world and theirs were one and the same, and he had simply been unaware of it up until now.

The door swung open, and the sensation grew so strong that Tyler took a step back to avoid being knocked off his feet. And he knew what it was.

Personality.

For an instant there in the driveway, edged up against a faded blue Volvo, he could feel the force of a personality shaped and infused by the power of individual souls linked together, still distinct yet One. It knocked the wind from his lungs.

"Won't you come in?" the young woman in the door asked.

Richard and Mary had already stepped inside. Chris was following but had paused on the doorstep to see what was keeping Tyler.

"Yeah . . . thanks, I'm coming," he managed.

The tidal wave of personality had somehow ebbed. He was aware of it still there, still surging in the air like water, but it was beyond his reach again. The house seemed quiet when he stepped inside.

Beyond a narrow entryway full of running shoes and rubber boots, lined with a long horizontal coat rack that was mostly empty thanks to the time of year, the house widened into a common room. It looked as though every possible wall had been knocked out in order to open up the floor. Couches, arranged in square configurations, surrounded several coffee tables. Chairs and reading lamps took up corners. There was plenty of floor space left over. Some of the seating was occupied; six people looked up with curious, welcoming eyes as the newcomers entered.

A middle-aged man wearing a grey sweater and glasses approached, holding out his hand. He shook Richard's hand warmly, greeted Mary like a long-lost sister, and welcomed Chris and Tyler. "I'm David," he said. "Please, come have a seat. Sharon's gone to make you coffee . . . or would you prefer something else?"

"Coffee's fine, thank you," Mary said, and the others nodded. "We can't stay long."

"Well, I must say I'm surprised to see you. It was good to hear your voice this morning, but I didn't think you were going to follow it up with a visit!" David's eyes twinkled as he ushered them to one of the couch-and-table clusters. A young man, about eighteen or nineteen, scuttled out of the way, taking a book with him. He gestured for Tyler to take his seat before vanishing into another room. "But don't take that as a hint. We would love to see more of you. You're an isolated crew."

"We try to stay focused," Mary said. "But maybe you're right. It's good to see you too, David."

She sat. Tyler noticed that she held herself erect, proud like a queen. She had been so worried and harried ever since he'd first met her that he hadn't noticed how attractive she was, or how much dignity there was in the small one's carriage. Something about her reminded him of Diane, and yet she was not like her at all. This was a woman who ran from nothing, who knew and had fully embraced her identity and purpose.

Another woman, who might have been David's wife—were any of these people married?—emerged carrying a mug of coffee in each hand; the eighteen-year-old whose seat Tyler had taken followed her with two more. They were handed to the guests, and the woman disappeared and quickly reappeared with another for David. Both vanished again, and Tyler noticed the other inhabitants of the room had likewise exited. He wondered why.

"Now then," David said. "I don't think you're here because the phone call made you miss the past. Can I help you with something?"

"I hope so," Mary said. Richard leaned forward slightly, as though he was expecting something to happen. Mary met David's eyes.

"I want you to tell me how to find the hive."

"Mary . . ." David drew the word out slowly. She watched him, searching his face, his body language, for any clue to his thoughts. They were Oneness, and they had a long history together, and yet she had never entirely learned to read him.

He sighed. "The hive is in our territory."

"We are Oneness," Mary said. "What is yours is also ours. I can't say I know why, but the plan seems to have led us here, David."

He raked a hand through his hair. "I am not trying to stop you. But the hive's power is not something to face unprepared. We've lost people. I told you."

"I have faced terrible things before," Mary said quietly. She kept her eyes fixed on his face, though he flicked his glance away. Some of those memories were shared. David had been there. The bombing, the fire. The hounding. Witchcraft unleashing violence and madness. The enemy was no trifling opposition.

Demons were just the beginning. What they could do in conjunction with humans was far, far worse.

The last two decades in the fishing village had been a welcome respite. Warm, quiet, a balance of sadness and victory. Nothing like the early days.

Not until April disappeared.

For a moment Mary let her eyes lower. She closed them and breathed a prayer for April. She was still convinced that her friend was not dead—and yet, in some strange way, the connection between them felt weaker than it ever had before. The sense of weakening was so clear as she reached out in spirit that she trembled inside.

April. April was why they were here.

"One of ours has gone missing," Mary said, raising her eyes again. "We've tried everything to find her. Things have been dark . . . she's been impossible to track. But I think the pieces are coming together now. I think the hive may be responsible for her disappearance."

"That does not necessarily mean you should go in," David pointed out. "Even if they did take her, it's unlikely they're keeping her here. Are you sure she isn't . . ."

"She isn't dead," Mary hastily answered. "Yet. Please, David, tell us what you know. We're not asking you to send anyone in with us. We only want to find out what we can learn."

David leaned back, resting his hand on the armrest of the couch he occupied alone. "I don't want to send you to your deaths. And it might well come to that. Mary, in twenty years I have never seen anything like this. It is far, far bigger than we can handle. We're in defensive mode—just trying to hold things together and beat back the darkness if it starts to spread. But we can't attack this. It would take a force a thousand times bigger than any cell." He glanced over at Richard, ignoring the boys. "A million times bigger than yours."

"Point taken," Mary said. "But you know the old saying: 'Despise not the day of small things.' We aren't going to attack. Just learn."

David shook his head. "You can't do it. You'll never even get in."

"We just need to know where it is, David."

He leaned back again and surveyed her carefully. Her inner response to his scrutiny was unexpected: for a moment she felt unsafe.

But that was nonsense. This man was Oneness.

And yet . . . hadn't he cut off Reese?

What kind of person would even think to do such a thing?

Taking a determined sip of coffee, Mary forced herself to shake off the thought and the premonition that had prompted it. It was only the memories that made her feel uncomfortable with him—the history they shared that both had spent two decades trying to forget. David had explained the exile. As far as he had been able to see, Reese was poison. And Mary hadn't met her—she had nothing to go on to the contrary but the word of two young men who were only just beginning to see hints of the world they blindly dwelt in.

David sighed again. Then he drew a piece of paper and a pen from his back pocket, bent over the coffee table, and jotted down an address. He handed it to her without a word.

"Thank you," she said, glancing at the address. Somewhere in Lincoln—she didn't know the city well enough to say exactly where.

"I can't send anyone with you," he said. "I'm sorry, Mary, but I can't be responsible for exposing more of our own. They are already too aware of us."

"I understand." She stood. "I don't know for certain what we're going to do when we get there anyway. No sense in you sending someone else to share in our uncertainty."

David stood as well, nodding at Richard, who joined them. "You have a man of prayer. At least you don't go unarmed. But these two now . . ." here his eyes moved to Chris and Tyler, who both took on a defensive stance. "These two have no armament at all, unless I am sorely mistaken."

She sighed. "You're not." Truth be told, she wasn't really sure why she had brought them here. To identify Reese if they found her, she supposed, and convince her to trust them. And because Patrick had spoken to Tyler. They clearly had a part in the plan.

"Why don't you leave them here?" David asked. "We'll look out for them until you come back." He left half his words unspoken. *If* you come back.

"Thanks, but no," Chris said. "I came along to help."

She breathed an inward sigh of relief that he said nothing more than that. The last thing she wanted was for David to know why they were really here—that they didn't expect to find April, but Reese. It wasn't that she didn't trust him, she told herself. It was just that he wouldn't understand. And whatever was going on with Reese, Patrick had indicated it was cloaked somehow. "Nothing is what it looks like," that was what Tyler had said was the message from the cloud. It wasn't David's fault if he couldn't see the truth.

Whatever the truth was.

Still, leaving the boys here didn't seem like a bad idea. She turned around to say so and saw the answer in Chris's eyes as clearly as if he'd been Oneness and they'd been closely connected enough to read each other's minds.

No.

Tyler, then. He was the younger and more vulnerable of the two anyway. But she opened her mouth to suggest he stay, and he met her eyes full-on and told her, silently, the same thing Chris had. He was coming.

Not, she realized, because of some macho bravado. Neither of the young men were here for an adrenaline rush or even to get answers for themselves—answers they deserved by now. They were here out of loyalty to a friend they barely knew.

She smiled and shook her head. "Thank you, David, but no. We'll watch out for them. I believe we'll be all right."

"You have more faith than I do."

She shook his hand, as did Richard after her. "We'll be careful."

Outside, on the sidewalk in front of the house, Mary let out a breath she hadn't realized she was holding. She looked down at the address in her hand.

"I forgot to ask him how to get there," she said.

"We'll find it." Richard's voice had a grim note to it. She looked at him, questioning. Yes, he'd felt it too . . . a need to hide. To keep their intentions secret. Coming to this house—when they'd walked up the driveway, the presence of so many other Oneness had wrapped both Mary and Richard and welcomed them home. So why their caution?

"I'm glad you're with me," she said quietly. He would know what she meant.

It was good not to rely on one's instincts alone.

The boys were already on their way back to the truck. Chris started to jog when he caught sight of someone leaning against the passenger door. Mary frowned. "Who . . ."

A step closer and she recognized him: the teenager from inside. Olive complexion and thick dark hair identified him as Mediterranean, maybe Italian or Greek. His back was to the truck and his arms wrapped across his chest.

He straightened up a little as they approached, and his eyes found Mary's.

She caught her breath. The boy's expression was tortured.

"Are you going after the hive?" he asked.

Mary looked over at Richard.

"Yes," he said.

"It's a warehouse where their power's located. A horrible place," the boy said. "Something happened there . . ."

"The exile?" Mary said quietly.

The boy's eyes widened. "You know about that?"

"David told us," Mary said. "A girl called Reese."

His expression grew more pained. "She was my friend. My sister and me, we went out on missions with her. I was with her . . . on the night they said she betrayed us."

Richard's brow darkened. "You sound like you don't agree."

The boy held out his hands beseechingly. "What do I know? Things went bad . . . Patrick got killed. But I never thought Reese was the problem. She thought she was doing the right thing. Following the Spirit."

A slight pang of guilt—the thought that David might not approve this conversation with a boy from his cell—twinged in Mary. But cell leaders weren't autocrats, after all. And the boy wanted to talk.

"Can you help us?" Mary asked. "Tell us how to get to this address?"

The boy glanced at the paper. "Yeah, I can take you there."

"Take us there?" Richard interjected. "You coming with us?"

The boy stepped away from the truck, unblocking access to the passenger's seat. "Yeah. If you're okay with that." He stuck out a hand. "My name's Tony."

"Good to meet you, Tony," Mary said, returning his greeting. His grip was strong, and knowledge of who he was flooded into her as their hands touched. Honest, brash, undyingly loyal. Oneness in every part of his being. Gifted—in warfare, she thought. Sword-handling, quickness. And there was something else.

She smiled, her heart quickening to an unexpected ache. "You're a twin."

"Yeah," he said. "Angelica—my sister—she's here with me."

"I was a twin," Mary said. "Long ago."

She repeated, "It's good to meet you."

Richard smiled suddenly. "Well, well," he said. Mary looked in the direction he was looking. A girl, Tony's age and strikingly like him in appearance, had stepped out from the other side of the truck.

"I want to come too," Angelica said. She shot Tony a look as he started to protest. "You left me behind last time. I hate being left behind."

Mary tuned the twins out as they argued with each other. As far as she was concerned, the question was settled. These two were a gift. They were coming.

* * * * *

The warehouse on Kliff Street looked, from the outside, like any other building in the industrial part of Lincoln. It was sandwiched between other warehouses, the outside facade corrugated tin painted a dull rust colour. Loading docks lined the back where Reese lingered in the shadows of a dumpster, watching.

Saturday morning, the industrial zone was quiet. No extra activity was happening here either—nothing to identify the warehouse as different from its neighbours. Even the spiritual darkness was remarkably damp—indistinct, low-lying, hard to sense. But then, that was a characteristic of this hive. It was better cloaked than any demonic operation Reese had ever encountered; it was part of how it had stayed undetected for so long, gaining an enormous foothold without the Oneness catching on.

It had been Reese who insisted there was more here than met the senses, something bigger going on than anyone realized. Reese who treated the war against this place as a full-scale assault—an offensive rather than ongoing defensive tactics. Reese who was sure she knew the way of the Spirit in this and had led teams in to follow that way.

Reese who had gotten Patrick killed and had inspired more conflict and dissension in the Lincoln cell than the Oneness had known perhaps ever.

She swallowed the lump in her throat. She couldn't dwell on the sorrow, on the grief, now. She had come here to die, but not without inflicting damage first. And she couldn't do that if she was emotionally incapacitated.

She felt weight, pressure, in the palm of her hand. Spirit gathered and concentrated its energy against that which was counter to it: against the dark powers of evil, hatred, and negation. The Spirit—life—found a thousand expressions in this world, but the one Reese wielded did more to express the potent reality of the world as it was than any other.

Sword.

They were at war.

An irony struck Reese: that as an exile, as one cut off from the Oneness and thrown into the world alone, she was acting toward the enemy as she had thought it was acting toward her: as a renegade. She would strike a blow for the sake of those she loved but was no part of.

Let me die in a blaze of love, she thought.

She stepped out from behind the dumpster in the oppression of memory, the trauma of victory ended in soul-cleaving defeat cutting at her heart. She stepped across the parking lot toward the inauspicious door next to a closed loading dock, carrying the absence of Tony and Patrick, the absence of the Oneness, with her—bearing the emptiness that undid her. But the sword was coming to hand, not denied her this one last time. She gripped it and pushed the door open.

The sound of empty, cobwebbed silence greeted her, the warehouse vast in its disuse. A cluster of pallets, six by six, stacked with cardboard boxes, sat in one corner. The rest of the empty concrete floor, shiny and smooth from the traffic of hundreds of feet, spread out from the door unencumbered and disappeared in shadows on all sides. On one high, wide wall, scrawled graffiti indicated that the warehouse had recently been broken into and vandalized. But there wasn't much here to vandalize.

The emptiness, like everything else about the hive and the creatures that powered it, was deceptive.

As she took more tentative steps into the gloom of the warehouse, Reese could feel the tension in the air, a low buzz growing with every inch forward. The sword took full form in her hand, slicing into visibility in the shadowed room. Slowly she became aware of a smell—a reek in the atmosphere, familiar, rotten.

She reached the middle of the floor and stood scanning the warehouse from wall to wall, floor to ceiling. Nothing moved.

They were here. Waiting.

For what?

She licked her lips and thought a final prayer.

Spirit, I come back to you. If you will take me, take me. If not . . . even so, I give myself to you.

Slowly they morphed out of the shadows. She saw them first as flickers, movements caught in the corner of the eye, flares of light—eyes glaring. The shapes gathered form, still vague as though she saw them through a screen.

"What are you waiting for?" she called.

No response, but the movements, the flickers, increased.

She stretched her arm out, holding the sword high. "I am alone," she called. "You remember me. I come alone, and I challenge you."

A creature over six feet in height, broad-shouldered like a man, melted out of the shadows directly across from her. Its face was a pair of eyes staring out of a mass of white scars.

"You," it rasped, "are not alone."

The words cut her to the heart.

And in her pain, she screamed out a battle cry and charged forward, swinging for the being's head. A sword of its own flashed out of the dark and met hers in the air, deflecting the blow and then slicing down at her. She ducked and spun out of the way, but the blade glanced her shoulder, cutting through her shirt and drawing blood.

Demons formed everywhere and charged from all sides. Reese fought like a wasp in a spider's web, entangled and doomed but determined to wreak as much destruction as she could. They hissed and shrieked and fell away from the bite of her sword, but there were so many. They were underfoot, tripping her up; latched onto her shoulders; biting at her neck and arms and legs. Fangs, razor claws, and the terrible chatter and noise of their words, ceaseless, pouring at her in a flood.

"Remove! Back, creatures of the dark!"

Another voice boomed through the warehouse and reverberated off the walls. From all around Reese it rose like a pillar of fire, thrusting her assailants away and flinging them to the ground and careening into the walls.

Reese turned to see a tall black man standing in the warehouse door with his hands lifted. His eyes and hands were blazing with light.

A man of prayer.

To her shock, Tony and Angelica appeared behind him.

Why were they here?

The demons regrouped and flew forward again, attacking both Reese and the newcomers in the door. Again the authority in the man's voice arrested their advance and flung them back. "Away, abominations!"

Reese gaped at the power the man displayed. The very air was vibrating and sparking with it. When the demons came forward once more and the man's voice boomed "Away!", the surge of power knocked her off her feet along with them.

She blinked up at the warehouse ceiling. Silence. The creatures had not re-formed this time. She could not tell if they were still there or if they had actually fled.

Everything hurt. Her neck and hands were sticky with blood. She was still clutching her sword.

A small woman knelt beside her—not old, but no longer young. Reese knew her for Oneness immediately. Her bearing and expression radiated wisdom and kindness.

But why were they here?

She licked her lips, tasting rust and dirt. The woman was smoothing Reese's hair back from her face and examining her wounds. Finally she said, "Are you all right?"

"I . . . I don't . . ."

Movement behind the woman drew Reese's attention. It was hard to see—harder to see than it should be. It took a moment to make sense of what she was seeing. But she managed to get out, "Chris?"

He said nothing. Just looked down at her with his protective, good heart in his eyes. And Tyler was there too—talking to her.

"Why did you leave? What were you thinking? You could have got yourself killed in here!"

Tony and Angelica's voices joined in, subdued but pressing her for answers too—wanting to know why she was here, wanting to know how she could still wield a sword, wanting to know if she was all right.

But it was the last of them that she wanted to see most, and it was he who appeared finally, standing over them all with an air of deep authority.

"Who are you?" she asked.

As though the others were not even there, he answered, "Richard."

And she knew that he could do what no one else could. This man who carried heaven's power in his voice could give her back what her heart wanted more than anything in this world—more than life, more than death.

"Tell me who I am," she said. Her voice sounded thick. The loss of blood . . .

He gazed solemnly down on her.

"You are Oneness," he said, and she closed her eyes and lost consciousness.

They hustled Reese out to the truck as quickly as they could without risking further injury to her and laid her down on the back bench. Richard motioned to the empty truck bed. "Get in," he told the younger crew. "We need to get away from this place."

Tyler and Tony nodded wordlessly. Chris fixed Richard with a glare, but the tall man laid his hand on the younger one's shoulder and said, "You ride in the bench. Keep Reese still. We're not trying to keep anything from you."

Chris nodded and got in without a word. Mary met Richard's eyes, pleading.

"I want us to get away from here," he repeated. "There is much more going on than what we saw in that warehouse."

"What I saw in that warehouse," Mary told him, "was the greatest show of power I have ever seen."

Weary to the bone, he nodded in acknowledgement. She

smiled, the corners of her eyes wrinkling. "And you told me April was more important than we knew." She took his hand and squeezed it tightly. "Whatever happens, my friend, I am proud to stand alongside you."

She let go and climbed into the cab. With a quick glance back at the warehouse to make sure nothing was coming after them—nothing visible, in any case—Richard put himself behind the wheel. Chris handed his keys up from the back bench.

"Where are we going?"

"Not far," Richard said.

"Back to the cell house?"

"No."

Richard shook his head as he turned the key and the engine ground to life. No, they were not going back there. It was the most natural place in the world for them to go: home to their brothers and sisters, home to the Oneness to combine their gifts and draw strength and healing from their Spirit connection.

But for the first time in his life, it was the wrong place to go.

"So," Mary said as they peeled onto the street and headed for the downtown core, "what was that place?"

"Murder, I think," Richard said. "The place reeked of it . . . or something like it."

"A serial killer?" Mary asked. "There were so many."

"I don't know."

Chris leaned forward from the backseat. "What are you talking about?"

"For a demonic core to grow to that size—and what we saw was just the tip of what was there, invisible—it needs a base in human evil. Something happened in that warehouse, or is still happening there, that gives them the ability to cluster in such numbers and also to take physical form like they did. Normally demons need to borrow bodies."

"I couldn't tell if they were physical, exactly," Chris said. "They looked so indistinct."

"That was as solid as they get on their own," Richard told him.

"So is that what you mean by a hive?" Chris asked. "A place where they can gather in large numbers?"

"No," Richard said grimly, "unfortunately, there is much more to it than that. What you saw was a core—a gathering of demons working together, feeding off the same energy source, united to some degree in purpose. The hive is not merely the core itself, but what they are doing with the power they're accessing."

"Which is . . .?"

"Possessing." Mary answered the question when Richard remained silent. "The demon that attacked in your house possessed a bat. But demons are strongest when they overtake people—when they have access to human intelligence, ingenuity, strength, and relationships. A hive is a network of human beings possessed and controlled by the demonic. They will work closely together and form a sort of community—it's a demonic mirror image of, and mockery of, the Oneness."

Chris sat back. "I can't imagine."

"You don't want to." Richard spoke again. "The Oneness is the ideal for mankind. Interconnectedness, gifts working in conjunction, an organic body—yet every one separate, unique, individual. Free. The strength of the Oneness is love, and love can only exist where freedom exists. A hive is different. It amalgamates—flattens its members into clones of each other. Its strength is not love, but repression. Sameness."

Mary wasn't sure why she said what she said next. "Your father—Douglas—was afraid of the Oneness because he thought we operated like a hive does. Yet the love he saw in us compelled him. I don't think he knew how to reconcile it with the ideas he already had about what it meant to be one of us."

"Did he ever do it? Become one of you?"

Mary looked down at her hands. "I'm not sure. I hope so."

"Because it means you'll see him again."

"Because it would mean we all will."

"Even me?"

Mary turned around. The young man's eyes were challenging her directly, a flare of independent thought demanding to be answered. Despite herself, she smiled at the sight of him—so exactly like Douglas, with his hand resting on Reese's head, stroking her hair and streaking his fingers with blood.

"This is what you want, you know," she said softly. "You've always wanted it. To save the world. To protect it. To be who you were born to be."

Did his hand shake? "I don't want to lose myself."

"We are not a hive."

"I don't know that."

She ducked her gaze from the desperation in his expression. "Then wait," she said. "Wait until you do know it. But don't wait too long. Others have waited too long."

When she glanced up again, he was staring out the window.

Richard checked his rearview mirror, his view of the road partially blocked by three young heads. The street was clear, the image of an industrial road on a weekend when the world was in bed or going to the bar. Sluggishly oblivious to all that was going on in higher realms around it. Sometimes, very rarely, he envied that kind of ignorance.

Now was not one of those times. What exactly the recovery of Reese meant he was not sure, but one element of it meant restoration, truth's triumph, and the healing of a splintered heart, and he was grateful with everything he was to have a part in that. He also knew, with the certainty born of prayer, that Reese was no exile. She was Oneness to the depths; always had been. Her willingness to die for the cause was only further proof of that.

But far from providing answers, that just furthered the mystery of what exactly had happened in this city—and what it had to do with the village, with April, with what all else this plan entailed.

Bombing up the road to a main artery of the city and then out to the freeway, Richard kept his eyes fixed ahead and let his heart reach out, up, wide and deep in prayer. It was harder now to concentrate than it had been when he chatted with Tyler in the backseat, but more important too. He nodded slightly to himself when the insight came; at least he knew where to go.

"How much longer, Richard?" Mary asked quietly. "She's

not doing well."

"Not far," he said. "I know where we're going."

"Tell me?"

"Tempter's Mountain."

"Ah. Are you sure?"

"Sure as sure."

Richard kept right through a highway split that took them completely out of Lincoln and turned them back toward the ridge that ran up the coast, back toward home. Their destination was a thirty-minute drive north of the village, the highest point of the ridge and lonely as any place along the bay.

"What's on Tempter's Mountain?" Chris asked. "You people got another cell up there?"

"Yes," Mary said, "in a manner of speaking."

"Can't be a very big one. Hardly anybody lives up there."

"It isn't," Mary said. "It's smaller than ours, as a matter of fact."

"And seldom visited," Richard added. He checked the rearview again. There were fewer cars on this freeway; less to watch; and that was putting him on edge in its own way. Solitary places could be the safest in the world. Or the most dangerous.

"And we are going there because . . ."

"Because that's what the Spirit is leading me to do," Richard said.

"Just you? Shouldn't you both have to agree on this? And those twins in the back?"

"Living in the Oneness is as much about trust as it is about agreement," Mary said. "We don't all need to come to an agreement, just to trust that the one who says he's hearing or seeing really is."

Chris fell silent again, and Richard flicked his eyes over to Mary's. She looked worried—concerned, Richard thought, not so much for Reese as for the questioning young man. They had some kind of story, Mary and the Sawyers. One day soon he figured she'd tell it.

A sudden loud thump on the roof of the truck caused Richard to jerk the steering wheel and then turn his eyes to the rearview again, pulling the truck back under control as he did. Tony was gesturing wildly for him to pull over.

"Trouble," Richard said.

In moments they were on the side of the freeway. No other vehicle was in sight. Richard jumped out and ran to the bed, followed by Chris.

"Up there!" Tony shouted, jumping out of the truck bed and landing in the gravel next to Richard. He pointed energetically at the sky. Dark clouds were gathering directly overhead, swirling in a distinctly unnatural way. There was no wind.

"Dear Lord," Richard said.

"What is it?" Chris asked urgently.

Richard shook his head slowly, eyes riveted to the swirling darkness. He could make out the edges of wings and claws in the swaths of cloud. "Chris, Tyler, get in the truck. Mary!"

Mary jumped out of the passenger's seat and looked at the sky. She put her hands together, and a long, black sword appeared between them. "Keep your eyes up," she instructed Tony and Angelica, who likewise took a defensive stance with swords in their hands.

Chris and Tyler hesitated.

"Boys, get in that truck," Richard said. "You can't fight this fight. Best way you can help us is to get yourselves out of harm's way."

The friends looked at each other, both uncertain. A smell was growing in the air, and a sound—a high-pitched, far-off sound growing in intensity.

"Get in the truck," Chris mumbled. He took his own advice, practically pushing Tyler in ahead of him.

Richard's eyes fixated on the cloud. "Ready . . . keep your eyes up and your hands steady . . ."

The first attack came shrieking out of the sky, eyes glistening, bearing long curved swords. They were coming down in demon form, the same indistinct and yet very real bodies that had attacked Reese in the warehouse. Whatever power was energizing the core, it was strong to give them this power so far from their base.

Tony yelled and jumped to give his sword more power coming down as the onslaught hit. Beside him, Angelica slashed the head off the first assailant to reach her. The two largest slammed into Mary and Richard, but both drove their swords deep into the creatures' chests, not even bothering to parry their swords. The demons were armed but attacked more like a pack of animals than like men: strength, teeth, speed, force. The Oneness dispatched the first wave quickly, but more were pouring down out of the cloud.

Inside the truck, the view had gone dark. Outside they could hear shrieking and what sounded like a gale wind; the truck rocked and shook with the force of it. Tyler and Chris had both crawled into the back bench and crouched on the floorboards, their heads ducked so they couldn't be seen easily from outside. They faced one another, questions in both their eyes.

A scream from outside. It might have been a woman. Chris's eyes flicked up. Something roared. A demon? Or Richard?

On the bench, Reese groaned and moved her head a little. Chris was immediately on the alert. "Hey, you waking up?" he asked softly. His question drew Tyler's attention.

Something slammed into the hood, and the truck rocked violently. Chris looked forward, but it was too dark to see—as though the truck had been plunged into a heavy fog.

"Listen, Reese," Tyler said, his voice urgent and just loud enough to be heard over the chaos, "I've got a message for you, and I don't know if I'm ever going to get a chance to deliver it. Patrick came to me . . . I guess you know who that is. And Richard already told you this, but I'm supposed to tell you too. You're not an exile. He said you were wrong about that. He said things aren't what they look like, and this is the kind of darkness that requires patience."

Tyler looked up anxiously as the noise grew once more and the truck lurched as though something huge had been hurled against it. Chris was tense, as though it was all he could do to stay here where he'd been sent and not throw himself out into the battle.

"Patience," Tyler repeated. "For the dark."

Reese opened her eyes and seemed to scrutinize him for a

moment. Her hand moved, and Tyler took it and squeezed it tightly. She managed a smile, but it was through tears, and the expression in her eyes was agonized.

"Thank you," she choked.

"Are we going to get out of here?" Tyler asked.

"I . . . don't know."

Chris started to rise. "That's it. I can't . . ."

Before he could finish his sentence, everything went silent.

A moment later the dark dissipated, vanishing like fog. The door behind Chris opened. Richard stood there, battered but definitely standing.

Chris turned himself around, half-standing. Richard saw the expression on his face. "It's all right," he hurried to say. "We're all fine. Just checking on you three."

"Better than ever," Tyler said, motioning down at Reese. Her eyes were closed again, but she looked a little less like she was lingering on death's door.

"Glad to see it."

"You're all okay?" Chris asked. He exited the truck. Mary, Angelica, and Tony were all on their feet, dusting themselves off, sporting bruises, scratches, and blood but not looking too much worse for wear. Mary smiled at him. "We're fine."

Chris looked up at the sky. The menacing clouds were gone entirely, replaced by the low sky of approaching evening. Tony slapped Chris's shoulder on his way back to the truck bed. "It was just a scrape," he said. "We've seen worse!"

Angelica winked as she followed her brother. "Only a little worse."

Bewildered, Chris looked again at Mary. "How was that not a lot worse than it was?"

"We're trained," she said, "and experienced, all of us. Those two troublemakers only look like children. They've been on fighting missions since they were in diapers. And the core was overextending itself. This is a long way from their base . . . they would have been better off possessing other bodies, but there's not much of use around here."

"This life is war," Richard explained. "Oneness don't have the luxury of overlooking that. We're always ready."

"Why attack you and not people like us?" Chris asked.

"They do attack you," Mary said. "In terrible ways. That's why we're here. To throw the fight back in their own faces. They won't attack you like that because it wouldn't help them to tip their hand." She laid a hand on his arm. Her knuckles were bloody. "We could always use another soldier."

Gently and respectfully, Chris removed her hand from his arm. He said nothing. But she understood, and he knew it.

He hoisted himself into the truck bed. "Tyler's turn to ride inside," he said.

* * * * *

The road up Tempter's Mountain was a dirt turnoff from the two-lane highway that had eventually taken the place of the freeway. It would be easily missed by anyone not looking for it. As it was, Richard drove past it and had to turn around, preferring not to slam on the brakes or make a hard turn with Reese in the back and his other passengers nursing their own minor wounds. Once on the road, he started the crawl up the steep hillside toward the peak.

"Haven't been here in forty years," he said.

Tyler leaned over the seat. "Where are we going?"

"A cell," Mary answered.

"In this wilderness? How many people live up here?"

Richard put the truck into third gear as the embankment grew even steeper. "Just one," he said.

They crawled around a corner, and a drop-off on their left revealed a breathtaking panorama of the bay and the ocean beyond. The blue sky, glistening clean and bright, stretched above forever, and a half-moon floated in the blue air.

"Good thing I'm not afraid of heights," Tyler said.

"What are you afraid of, Tyler?" Mary asked.

Tyler's voice softened. "Don't really make small talk, do you?"

"Not particularly, no."

He kept his eyes fixed on the water and the moon. "Lack, maybe. I think I'm afraid of not having enough." He paused. "That I've never had enough. That I'll never have what I really need . . . what I'm looking for."

"And what is that?" Mary asked.

"I don't know for sure."

The road took another sharp bend, this time putting the

bay behind them and plunging the truck into a tangle of twisted trees and scrub bushes that looked like they'd been waging a battle to take over the road. Someone had patiently cut them back, leaving a path wide enough for the truck to drive through without a scratch. The ground levelled, and ahead of them appeared a small house set against another embankment, overshadowed by two huge old pines and landscaped with little more than sandy dirt and rocks. But it was kept neatly enough.

Richard put the truck in park and turned off the ignition.

"Well?" Mary asked.

"The trees are taller. Other than that it looks exactly the same."

She opened her door first. "I wonder whether we're expected."

Richard followed her out, pausing to tell Tyler, "Stay put." He rested his hand on the edge of the truck bed. "You three had best stay here until we make sure we're not too much of an intrusion."

Dirt and gravel crunched under their feet as Richard and Mary made their way to the front door. He knocked, and they waited.

The door swung open, and an ancient, cavernous face looked up at them from a body that was nearly ninety years old and under five feet tall. Yet the eyes were bright and the welcome real.

"More company, eh?" the old hermit croaked.

Richard smiled. "Do you remember me?"

"Sure I do." The hermit tapped his temple. "I don't forget.

You're . . . Robert."

"Richard."

"Richard, of course. And you I don't know."

"Mary."

"Welcome, welcome. You got more out in that truck?"

Tony's head was peering up over the cab, and the hermit waved at him.

"If we're not too much of an imposition," Richard said.

"Not at all." The hermit stepped back and swung his door all the way open. He gestured broadly for the others to come in and watched as the twins and Chris piled out of the bed. Tyler jumped out of the backseat, and Chris climbed halfway in. He emerged a moment later carrying Reese. The twins nodded to the hermit as they entered, and he clapped each of their arms like they were long lost grandchildren. Tyler followed, joining the twins in the narrow entryway that led to a living room tinier than the one at the boys' cottage.

Chris approached the doorstep, and the hermit's eyes fell on Reese. Suddenly his posture went rigid, and his face grew dark. He looked up at Richard, his eyes accusing and intense.

"What are you doing? Why have you brought this here?"

Richard and Mary exchanged a confused look, and Richard searched for words.

The hermit cut him off. "Can't you feel what's in front of your face, man? This girl is an exile!"

Chris stopped, refusing to take another step. It wasn't clear that the hermit would have allowed him entrance anyway, as long as Reese was in his arms. Richard interposed himself between them.

"Respectfully, sir, she isn't," he said.

The hermit turned blazing eyes on the younger man. "Do you think your senses are sharper than mine? I've been honing them for seventy years!"

"Up here?" Richard shot back. "I'd think being alone so long might dull things."

"Richard," Mary said sharply, laying her hand on his arm. He bowed his head. "I'm sorry. That was out of line. But sir, this girl isn't an exile. We thought so too, but . . ."

The hermit took a step forward, nearly pushing Richard aside, and glowered down at Reese. Chris stood tense but didn't back away. "I only know what I feel," the hermit muttered. "I didn't think exile was possible, but this . . . can't you feel the poison? The death radiating from her?"

"I feel the grief," Mary said.

"Sir, I've been in prayer for days, and I've seen this girl in action. She wields a sword and is willing to give herself up for the Oneness. Whatever you're feeling, it isn't real."

The hermit shook his wizened head, still staring intently at Reese. "I don't like this."

"Is it possible that you're sensing a cloak?" Mary asked. "A deception?"

The hermit raised his eyes to her. "It's too strong for that. Too real. And how could you possibly cast a cloak like this unless . . ." He shook his head vehemently. "You'd have to project it. It's not possible."

"Nevertheless," Richard said, putting a hand on Chris's shoulder and giving him a look that said Stay put, "she's badly hurt. We brought her here looking for help. Even if she is an enemy, surely you agree that we should help her?"

The hermit shook his head as though to dislodge something and muttered a few words to himself, then out loud said, "Of course. Bring her in."

Objecting with his eyes but not with the rest of his body, Chris carried Reese past the hermit and laid her on a couch in the tiny living room. Strong light poured in through the window. The hermit examined her quickly and cursorily.

"You," he said, summoning Angelica with his eyes, "go in the kitchen and look in the third cupboard for a tall green bottle. It's got something that will help start her off to healing, at least. But these wounds are bad. How'd she get them?"

"Went into a fight with the demonic," Richard said. "A core. She fought them directly."

The hermit looked impressed. "And you got her out?"

"I told you I've been in prayer. For days. I had enough power to knock them off her long enough for us to grab her and run."

He shook his head again. "I don't like any of this. And I've got bad news for you. I can start her off to healing, but she needs more than I can do for her."

Angelica appeared carrying the old bottle, and the hermit took it with thanks and screwed the cap off, pouring a little of the liquid into it. "Help me," he said, and Angelica knelt beside Reese and helped the old man get the liquid past her lips.

"She needs to be taken to a hospital," Mary said, looking to Richard for confirmation.

He shook his head. "I don't think that's an option. The hive will be looking." He fixed his eyes on the hermit, but the old man ignored him.

Mary nodded, turning the options over in her head. "We can get an IV . . . bring it up here. I know how to use it." She turned her eyes on the hermit. "If we can get supplies, will you let us treat her here?"

"It's a matter of life and death," Richard put in. "If we take her into a public place, I have no doubt the demons will find her and kill her. They've been after her for days, and it's all been aggravated now."

"Fine," the hermit said. "I'll make a list . . . tell you what to get if you can get it. Send those young people off in your truck for it. I'd rather you stayed here and kept an eye on her."

"She is trustworthy," Richard said.

The hermit met his eyes finally and sighed. "No. She is not."

"You're believing a lie."

"I'm believing the only thing I can feel. When you're alone as long as I've been, boyo, you learn to trust your own instincts."

✳   ✳   ✳   ✳   ✳

Richard gave the orders. Tony and Angelica looked unhappy to be sent off, but they took the turn of events as a matter of course. Tyler and Chris put up more of a fight. Both wanted to stay with Reese. The twins could find medical supplies on their own, and besides, if demons attacked again, the village lads would be less than useless.

Richard frowned. "No," he said after the boys had finished their protest. "I think it's best you go. Head for the clinic in the village. They'll have what we need. Best to stay out of the city. Chris, your mother can help . . ."

"No," he said. "I don't think so."

"Mary told me she was a nurse," Richard said. "The clinic will give her supplies. How are you planning to get them otherwise—steal them?"

The twins exchanged guilty glances. Richard fixed them a stern glare. "No. Go to Chris's mother. She'll help you."

"She won't," Chris said.

Richard turned his eyes on the young man. "Chris, I know you don't like any of this, and I know you're trying to protect your mother. But she is one of us, and right now we need her. You know she won't turn us away this time. She's a good woman. We've asked her for very little—I didn't even know about her until all this began—but this time we have to. You can help us best—Reese as well as the rest of us—by going to her."

Conflict tore Chris's face. He opened his mouth to say something but thought better of it. "Fine. We'll get the supplies. Tell me again why we can't take her to the city where someone will actually care for her?"

"I don't think the city is safe," Richard said. "She's a target, and the hive could be anywhere—it may even have spread outside of Lincoln."

"And you think she's safe here? On top of a mountain with no one around but an old man who thinks she's poisonous? If you're attacked here . . ."

"The Spirit led us here," Richard said. "And that old man is no ordinary octogenarian. This may be the safest place we could possibly be." He sighed. "I'm as unhappy as you are about the hermit's reaction to Reese, but he'll see the light in time. He's right about one thing—whatever is cloaking her, it's powerful. I don't understand where its power is coming from. I promise, Chris, I will find out what it is and learn how to break it. For now, you can trust the hermit not to harm her."

Chris balled his fists, but he nodded and turned to go. The others were already waiting at the truck.

Behind Richard, the hermit appeared in the door and called after Chris, "Don't resist forever, boy. There's too much to do."

Chris looked back and scowled, not slowing his march to the truck.

"Don't wait," the hermit repeated. "Just you remember that. You wait too long, you lose opportunity that won't ever come back."

Chris just turned his face away and jumped into the truck, starting it with a roar.

"I'm sorry," Mary said, joining the hermit. "That was a bit rude. He's . . ."

"I know what he is," the hermit said. His voice was intense, but not offended—and his eyes were still fixed on Chris as the truck barrelled off the property. "I know just what he is."

* * * * *

Tears slipped from beneath Reese's eyelids as she listened to the men argue in the next room. The hermit and Richard were discussing her again, and their voices were growing heated. Each man sure of what he knew. Each man sure of what the Spirit had told him.

She was causing dissension again.

She'd been awake the whole time—since slightly before their arrival on Tempter's Mountain. But it was easier to keep her eyes closed and pretend she heard nothing. To let them attribute the pain that crossed her face to her physical wounds, which were, admittedly, bad. A bite in one shoulder felt hot, and a deep scratch in her side was still bleeding, or at least she thought it was.

But she could probably walk. Even throw herself back into battle if she had to. Part of her had insisted she do so: sit up and tell Chris she could walk on her own, could carry her head high into the hermit's cottage even against his protestations against her presence.

It felt better to be carried.

The loss she felt when Chris set her down and turned away was sharper than she wanted to admit. She was amazed, in a way, that she could feel it—but then, she was good at feeling loss. One after another.

The truth was, horrible though it was to admit, if she was pressed she would agree with the hermit. He was right and Richard was wrong, no matter how much authority she had heard thundering in his voice in that warehouse. Tyler was wrong—what could he really know? He wasn't even Oneness.

She wanted to believe them, tried to believe them, but when she reached out in tentative hope she felt only the same roaring emptiness and grief on all sides of her spirit. If they were right—if her bearing the sword meant something, if she was cloaked somehow, if she was really still Oneness—then why couldn't she feel the truth of their words?

But Tyler had known about Patrick. How could he, if it was all a lie?

Her thoughts were interrupted by a growing sense that something was very, very wrong.

And she heard a voice.

"Reese."

She turned her head and looked toward the window. There was another door there, heading outside, and to her surprise, it was standing partially open. But she couldn't see the source of the voice.

"Reese," it called again, more insistently this time.

"Patrick?"

She pushed herself up to a sitting position. The room spun and darkened for a moment, and she closed her eyes to give herself time to adjust. The argument in the other room was growing louder. She heard Mary's voice, pitching in with less vehemence. How grateful she was for these two—for Oneness who stood by her, who wanted to believe in her.

Even if they were wrong.

As soon as she thought she could manage, she stood and crossed the room, hand on the wall, and peered out the window. Nothing. No one.

". . . only until she can walk," the hermit said. "This place is shielded, but I'm not sure what bringing something like her here will do to the shield. If her presence tears a hole in it, we might be vulnerable to attack even now."

"We'll fight if they come here," Richard said.

Reese closed her eyes. Yes, they would. At what cost?

She didn't know—couldn't know—the answer to the question they debated. But that she represented a danger was not a question in her mind. Demons had attacked her in the village, in the city, and on the road.

They had saved her life, and she was grateful. But she wasn't their responsibility anymore. Not any of them—not the boys, not the village cell, not the hermit.

It was time to go.

* * * * *

Chris guided the truck expertly down the cliff roads, handling hair-raising curves and dusty potholes with equal aplomb. Tyler sat next to him, the twins behind, hanging on to the back of the seats in front of them with their eyes shining. The sun overhead poured down over the vast blue expanse of the bay.

The village roads forced Chris to slow down, but Tyler could tell his friend was taking them as fast as his conscience would allow. They pulled into the driveway behind Diane's house, sandwiched in with other tall, narrow houses on a road that overlooked the water, and Tyler put his arm on Chris's.

"Wait," he said. "Who's here?"

Chris had already noticed. A black car was parked in Diane's driveway, and her curtains were drawn. Without a word, he threw the truck back into gear and backed out fast, roaring down the street in the direction they had come.

"Why are we leaving?" Tony asked from the back.

"Hoping they'll think we were just turning around," Chris said.

"They?"

"Whoever is paying my mother a visit."

Chris set his jaw grimly, and satisfied that the truck was out of sight of the house, he pulled into the vacant driveway of a house that looked closed up for the moment and sat, his hands on the wheel, immobile.

"Dang," he said. "Dang it."

"Who do you think they are?" Tyler asked.

"I don't know," Chris said. "And I know everyone my mother

knows. I've never seen that car before."

Chris turned and regarded the twins, who were listening and watching silently but were still tensed forward like a pair of cats ready to spring. "If we get near the house," he said, "can either of you . . . tell things?"

Angelica raised both eyebrows. "Meaning?"

"My mother has instincts," Chris said. "Impressions and visions and things like that. Like you all . . . like Richard and Mary. Do you? If we get you close to that house, will you be able to tell what's going on inside?"

"We're not magicians, man," Tony said.

"We're not eyes, either," Angelica hurriedly added. "Which is I think what you're asking. Sorry . . . our gift is fighting. Swordplay."

Tyler recalled the battle with the demons that had swooped on the truck and nodded. "Lucky you were with us back there," he said, knowing even as he did that luck had nothing to do with it. It was Oneness. It brought all the necessary parts together when they were needed, where they were needed, like a body calling up its various powers to see in the dark, or hear whispers, or react instinctively.

"But whatever's going on," Tony said, "you know we'll help you. You and your mother. Whatever you need."

Chris looked at Tony like he was seeing him for the first time. "Do you know who my mother is?"

Tony glanced at Angelica, and they both shrugged.

"Never mind," Chris said. "Thank you. I'm going back there now."

"No, you're not," Tyler said. "I am."

Chris regarded him like he'd grown another head. Tyler sat up a little straighter. He did not usually challenge his friend—definitely did not tell him what he could or could not do. But this time he knew he was right.

"It's your mother in there. I don't trust you to keep your head. If everything isn't just fine, I can keep my cool enough to pretend to be the newspaper boy or something, come to collect dues. It won't necessarily tip them off. And we can make a plan before we just go in fighting."

No one asked why everyone was assuming that the black car in Diane's driveway meant bad news. With everything else that was happening, it seemed the safest assumption.

"Fine," Chris said. "Go to the door and find out what you can. We'll be right behind you if you need us. Out of sight."

Tyler nodded and opened the truck door. He ducked out into the bright sunshine and jumped down. The cobbled road leading back to Diane's was quiet as he trudged up it, trying to keep his nerves steady. A sense of foreboding grew. He knew the others were behind him but couldn't see them and tried not to hear them. He fixed his eyes ahead, on the tall white house with the black car in the driveway.

What are you doing? he asked himself.

I'm not sure, he answered. Just trying to help.

You're playing Oneness, came a voice back.

He was, too. Trying to be the part that was in place at just the right time, trying to be the one who filled a need. Need frightened him. It had frightened him from the day his parents died. All of life seemed a gaping hole, a lack so palpable it could swallow him. With Chris, with his friendship, he ran from that. He filled it with quiet, and fishing, and a surrogate family in the Sawyers. But the Oneness was something more than friendship, more than family. It was not threatened by need. It could not be swallowed by lack. It swallowed lack instead—swallowed it in a sufficiency and companionship and interrelatedness that was more than he had imagined could exist.

Playing Oneness, he reminded himself.

And there, six steps from Diane Sawyer's kitchen door, he imagined what it would feel like to stop playing. For a moment he dreamed that the world hazed behind a grid, a web, a tapestry of threads in perfect order, and then the grid disappeared and the world was back, but not the same. He imagined himself gasping as he could feel them—Tony, Angelica, Diane—their personalities surging into his, their minds and spirits alive and present to him. Not merging with his—separate and distinct. And yet part of him too.

For a brief second his imagination expanded, and he felt what it would feel like to know a thousand—a million—millions—of minds and hearts and spirits and gifts, all part of him, all connected to him. And it was as though they all were smiling, and all were saying, "Welcome home."

"It's real, you know," a voice beside him said.

Tyler nearly jumped out of his skin. The tall, big figure of a man who had appeared to him in the cliffs with a message for Reese was standing beside him. The man, Patrick, didn't look quite so battered and bloody this time, as though he'd found a few minutes somewhere to clean up. If a ghost could clean up. He was huge and tough and intimidating. And yet veiled somehow.

"Well?" Patrick asked. "Are you waiting for something?"

"I . . ." Tyler closed his mouth. "I'm . . . what are you doing here?"

Patrick chuckled. "Let's just say I'm along for the ride." He gestured at the house. "You really wanna know what this life is all about, keep walking. That's the only way you learn any-thing—by experience and carrying on."

Tyler nodded, decided to temporarily ignore the fact that he was talking to a ghost, and kept on toward the door.

He knocked.

It was a moment before anyone answered, but the door on the other side of the screen unlatched and opened about an inch. A man, short and covered in tattoos, peered out. "Yeah?" he asked. "Can I help you with something?"

Tyler cleared his throat. "I wondered if Mrs. Sawyer was in. Paper boy . . . it's dues day."

Trying not to be too obvious, he did his best to peer around the man into the house. But it was no good. The man wasn't big, but he was effectively blocking every inch of visibility, and he seemed in no hurry to open the door wider.

"She's occupied," the man said. "Got guests. Can you come back?"

"Well, it would be a pain," Tyler said. "I've got a whole route to do, and then I'd have to walk all the way back . . . I'll just be a minute. Can I see her, please?"

The man looked behind him as though to confer with someone else. Tyler heard nothing—no whisper or conversation—but the man turned back to him and said, "No. She says she's busy. Look, kid, come back tomorrow. This ain't a good time."

Tyler nodded. "Right. Thanks for your time."

He turned away and heard the door bang shut behind him. To his surprise, Patrick was still standing at his side. The man—or ghost, whatever he was—looked grim. He walked companionably alongside Tyler as they strolled back up the road, trying not to look too hurried. Finally, out of sight of the house, Chris, Tony, and Angelica appeared. Where they had been hiding was anybody's guess. They were good at this, Tyler thought.

"Well?" Chris asked. His tone was sharp, and his eyes bored right through his friend.

"They wouldn't let me in. I think she's there . . . but they're not friendly."

"You're sure of that?" Chris asked.

"I saw one of them through the window," Angelica said. "Big man, shaped like a hammer. I'd know him anywhere. He comes to visit David. He's Oneness."

"He's not," Tyler said, amazed at the surety in his own voice. "He's not. Can't be." He looked to Patrick for confirmation and realized the big man had vanished—or just gone back behind the veil. How this cross-mortality business worked was beyond him.

"I'm sure he's Oneness," Angelica repeated. "David trusts him."

"But you can't feel him?" Tyler pressed. "I mean, like Chris asked before . . . can't you just tell if someone is Oneness or not?"

She shrugged. "Yes, if I really think about it . . . but it's not always sharp from a distance. Why are you so sure he can't be one of us? This is good news!"

"I'm sure whoever's in that house, they're not good news. I might not be Oneness, but even I can get a gut feeling about something."

"Hey," Tony interrupted. "Heads up."

The others looked at him, and he pointed to the street they had all just stepped off of. A boy, maybe ten or eleven years old, was wandering up it pushing a bike, looking intently around him as though he was hunting for someone. His hair was sandy blond, his face pinched and aged beyond its years.

Tyler cast a glance at the others and then stepped out into the street. "You looking for something?" he asked.

The boy lit up at the sight of him. "Yeah, you!"

He pushed his bike close at a jog and then stopped inches from Tyler, looking around furtively as though he was afraid someone was following him. The boy lowered his voice. "You were just at the white house up the street."

"Yeah, I was," Tyler said. He dropped to one knee to be eye-to-eye with the boy, who was small for his age. "What about it?"

"I don't know," the boy said, and Tyler realized he was shaking. "I think something bad is going on there. Hey, if I'm wrong, you won't tell nobody, will you?"

Tyler reached out and lightly rested his hand on the boy's shoulder. "No, no, of course not. What's got you spooked?"

"Some men went in there this morning," the boy said. "I saw them."

"They're just visiting," Tyler said cautiously. The boy shook his head, his blond hair in vehement disarray. "No, I seen them before. Down at the dock—" The boy shook even harder, and his eyes filled with tears. "I know I shoulda told somebody . . . I shoulda gone to the cops. But I was scared . . . I didn't know what to do."

"It's okay," Tyler said, now stroking the boy's head. He realized he was treating him like a much younger child, yet the boy didn't shy away from his touch. It was as though he desperately needed a mooring, a secure place, and he had found it and latched on to it in Tyler.

"There was a lady," he said. "My friend. She came down to the docks where I read my books and was talking to me. Those men—" he pointed up the road toward the house— "they took her."

Tyler's blood ran cold. "When?"

"Thursday morning," the boy said.

These were the men who had taken April.

"Thank you," Tyler told the boy, processing the news as fast as he could think. "You were brave to tell me. What's your name?"

"Nick," the boy said.

"Listen, Nick," Tyler said quietly, "can you go home? Are you safe there?"

The boy's mouth twisted a little, but he nodded.

"Okay," Tyler said. "Go home. Thank you for what you told me. It's going to save somebody else."

The boy's eyes filled with tears, and he nodded again. Tyler's heart lurched as he stood and pulled his hand away from the dirty hair. "You'd better get going," he said. "Everything's going to be fine. You did the right thing. Understand?"

The boy nodded one more time, then hopped on his bicycle and pedalled away. Tyler stood in the street, looking after him and noting the direction he rode. Then he turned. The others were right behind him, Chris closest of all.

"They're the men who took April," Tyler said. "The boy saw it."

"I don't understand," Angelica said. "They're friends of David's! What . . ."

Tony put his hand on his twin sister's arm. "We've known all along something wasn't right," he said. "Maybe we're starting to find out what."

"What do we do now?" Tyler asked.

"Go to Richard," Angelica said, at the same moment that Chris said, "Rescue my mother."

* * * * *

Once outside the door, Reese let her legs take her. She moved blindly, following trails at the back of the house into the cliffs. It struck her that they couldn't be far from the village—the bay was far below, down steep cliffs. The terrain was steeper and more frightening here, but traversable. It reminded her of the place she'd tried to kill herself.

There was no sign of Patrick, and she wondered if she had imagined the voice. Either way, she was glad she'd left. The argument was behind her, and she was alone with her grief again. It was becoming a familiar companion, one that she didn't like to share with anyone else. She suspected she had put the hermit's protective shield behind her, but she couldn't feel it . . . all of her senses, once alive to connection, were dead.

"Why am I alive?" she heard herself asking. But no answer came.

How long she stumbled along the paths she didn't know, but eventually she spotted a cave.

A dark shadow in the cliff side below a bluff, accessed by a narrow, precarious trail, was all that marked its location. She was above it, and it would be hard going to get down. Besides, with the warm sun on her back as she climbed the trail and the sight of seabirds diving and circling in the air beyond the cliff, she had little desire to plunge herself into the dark. She intended to keep going, get as far away from the hermit and the cell members as she could before her groaning, protesting body collapsed.

And she would have done so, if she hadn't seen the woman.

A woman stood in the path just in front of the entrance to the cave. Beautiful, with long dark hair and a cream-coloured dress that reached to her ankles, she looked as though she had stepped out of another time.

Her eyes were fixed on Reese.

The woman raised her hand and beckoned Reese to come.

And then she vanished.

Reese stood blinking and wondering what she had just seen. The cloud? Why here?

She wouldn't know if she didn't try to find out.

One slow, careful step at a time, Reese made her way down to the path and the entrance of the cave. When she reached the entrance, the sense of power in the air nearly knocked her off her feet. This, she could feel. Evil—but not just evil. Other powers had met here, had clashed perhaps, and all had left their mark. The woman from the cloud might have had something to do with it.

At the moment Reese stepped over the threshold of the cave, the reek slammed into her, turning her stomach. The small hole in the cliff opened into a biggish room that narrowed down to another hole, and this was one was blocked by iron bars.

A door. A prison.

"What is this place?" she breathed.

The answer came to her. A killing cave.

Reese looked around and spotted a torch and matches. Someone had been here not long ago—or the woman from the cloud had managed to bring supplies here. She was more open to the first option. Lighting the torch, she held it high, trying to ignore the smell. The iron bars seemed rusted but strong. A lock made it clear that anyone behind the door was not meant to come out. There was no key that she could see.

It can be picked.

Was that a woman's voice?

Regardless, picking locks was something she could do. She put out the torch and staggered back out into the bright sunlight to search for a suitable tool, wondering all the while exactly what she thought she was doing.

She was supposed to be running away. Not getting all wrapped up in opening a door.

Then again, maybe this was part of a plan.

That thought kept her going. Twigs and pine needles were useless, but she found a piece of wire in a bird's nest, conveniently located in the cliff side where it wasn't hard to reach, and silently thanked whoever exactly was guiding her before returning to the cave and picking the lock. She relit the torch and pushed open the door.

The smell grew stronger, and she held her breath for a moment before realizing she couldn't keep that up and settled for breathing through her mouth. Dim light filtered in from outside, and she could hear water dripping somewhere. She held the torch up and peered through the gloom, sure she was supposed to see something.

She did, although it took a moment to realize she was looking at a body.

"Oh, God." She dropped to her knees beside the form curled up in a corner of the cave. The torch spread light on a girl, about Reese's own age, gaunt and pale and dirty. Light blonde hair fell around her face and partially obscured the black ink of a rose vine tattooed across one shoulder.

She was breathing, Reese realized with simultaneous relief and fear. Not conscious, but alive.

And almost certainly, her name was April. This was the girl Mary and Richard were searching for.

In her mind she turned the events, the words, the revelations of the last few hours. A few rang over and over, offering life that Reese could not quite seem to grasp. But this was part of a plan. It had to be. And if she could still wield a sword—and speak with the cloud—and be drawn this deeply into a plan so tangled and full of power . . .

You are Oneness. Richard had said it. Even the demons had said it. Not an exile. It was not true. She was not alone.

But somehow her heart hadn't come back to life at the words. Could it be so dead—so broken—after the pain of the deception that it wasn't possible to revive it?

Richard's words, spoken with authority, meant the most. But it was Tyler's, offered in a faithful panic, that were strengthening her now. Listen, Reese. You're not an exile. Patrick said you were wrong about that. He said things aren't what they look like, and this is the kind of darkness that requires patience.

Patience. The word meant endurance—the strength to continue, to not give up, to not stop fighting, not stop waiting, not stop believing. Patience for the dark. The hardest, and most important kind. Patience to continue when there seemed to be no reason to do so.

To keep living in a place like this, where someone had left you to die.

"This is about you, isn't it?" Reese asked the unconscious girl. "You need it too . . . patience. Seems like you have it. But I hope your dark is over. I hope if you wake up, when you wake up, everything is right for you. Everything is . . . healed."

April made no response, and Reese felt the presence and possibility of death like a noxious fume in the air.

But then she heard the voice again—the voice that might be a woman's, might be from the cloud, or might just be her own imagination.

Hold the torch high, and look around you.

The light of the torch, for a moment, did more to cast shadows and confusion than to illuminate. But Reese slowly rose, holding it still and high, and as her eyes focused, she caught her breath—for a very different reason this time.

"Incredible," she muttered.

April had done this?

Revealed in flaring, living reality by the light, paintings covered every visible inch of the walls and ceiling. In character they reminded Reese of pictures of prehistoric cave paintings—April's materials had been similar, apparently just red mud and the natural shapes and colours of the rock—but with far more detail. Rose vines grew, arched, and coiled throughout the mural, thorny and flowering.

But this wasn't just about art.

The woman was there, beautiful and grim. "Do you see it?" she asked.

For a moment, Reese didn't.

And then she did.

"The truth revealed," the woman said.

Painted across the wall in excruciating detail was Reese's own story.

And with it, the secret of the hive.

The discovery that Reese was gone sent Mary and Richard into desperate searching. The hermit responded grimly, confirming his own opinion of her trustworthiness—clearly she was stronger than she'd allowed them to see and had been deliberately deceiving them. His best guess was that she'd come here to tear the shield or lead the demonic to his hiding place. Richard ignored his suggestions and hunted through the bush with Mary at his side, eventually wending their way up the bluffs behind the house and into a thicket of thorny bushes. It looked like Reese had been this way. The hermit trailed behind them, offering suggestions and occasionally water.

They hadn't been in the thicket more than five minutes when the sound of a car pulling up to the house set Mary on high alert. She could just see the driveway from here, and she focused her eyes on it while staying low, hoping it was Chris and Tyler and the others—although this was too early, too soon for them to be back.

It wasn't them. It was a green station wagon she had seen before. Relief flooded her, mixed with an unexpected caution.

David's car. The Oneness was here.

"My God," the hermit breathed. It was a prayer, not an expletive. "How have they come here?"

The two men and Mary had just rounded the corner to the house in time to see the car and David pushing his way through the front door, accompanied by four other men. Mary started forward to greet them, but Richard grabbed her arm and motioned for her to keep silent. They ducked back out of sight and found themselves a place from which to watch.

"They're human," Richard said grimly. "Your shield can't keep them out."

"I don't understand," Mary said. "David is one of us. Why aren't we . . ."

"He is," the hermit said. "Those others aren't. The men with him are possessed."

"They . . ." Mary stopped. "What?"

"This may be why Reese ran," Richard said quietly. "She may have sensed them coming."

"This doesn't make sense," Mary said.

"Little has, lately."

The men seemed to be searching the house. Crouching at Richard's feet, Mary closed her eyes. She focused on the Spirit all around, on the power holding the world together, on the closeness of Richard and the hermit, on their combined strength. She focused and brought all these things together in the palm of her heart and lifted them in prayer.

The sensation came in a rush—expansion, contact. Eyes and ears.

Mary gasped.

Reese was nearby.

And April.

* * * * *

"I'm not waiting," Chris said. "I don't care what anyone says. My mother is in there with a couple of kidnappers, and I am not walking away without her."

He was staring down Tony and Angelica, who had both insisted—and continued to insist—that they needed to wait for Richard. To drive the truck back to the hermit's and tell him and Mary what had happened, and to come back in greater force, with the man of prayer and the leader of the village cell both with them. They didn't know what they were facing here, but it was more than just demonic, and the twins weren't confident of their ability to handle it. Better that they wait and do this properly.

Tyler had never felt so torn.

He had known Chris all his life. They were closer than brothers. It was Chris who had drawn Tyler into his world, had provided him with security, with friendship, with a place to call home. He had even shared his mother—Diane, who was in trouble now. But Tony and Angelica were part of a world Tyler desperately wanted to understand, a world he was beginning to trust more than his own. He saw the world as bigger than Chris did, understood that all this mess was far, far more than this single moment. That it was bigger than just one person or one threat.

"We need to wait," Angelica stressed again. "They went after your mother because she's Oneness. This is a strike on all of us. It's foolish to try to do this on our own. It's one thing to fight demons, but this time there are people involved. We have to be careful."

"You followed Reese, didn't you?" Chris asked. "When she wanted to do something foolish on her own and attack that hive? Isn't that why some of you people threw her out?"

Tyler grimaced at the harsh words and the harsher tone. "Chris . . ."

Chris rounded on him. "That's my mother in there, Tyler! She needs us now!"

"You're right," Tyler said, trying to swim his way through a sea of conflicting thoughts and emotions. "You're right. She needs us. We need to help her."

He turned to Tony and Angelica and repeated the words, beseeching: "We need to help her."

"You don't need their permission," Chris snapped.

To both their surprise, Tony stepped between them and said, "All right. So what do we do?" He nodded to Chris. "You're in charge. Tell us what to do and we'll do it."

Angelica stifled a protest. Chris raised an eyebrow. "You're following me? I'm not one of you."

"Doesn't matter," Tony said. "Right is right. I'd like to wait for Richard, but you can't, I can see that. So we'll stand with you. Tell us what to do."

Chris seemed taken aback, and for a moment he sought for words. "The attic," he finally said. "There's a door on the roof that leads into the attic. From there we can come down the back stairs and into the house. Tyler can go back to the door—pretend he decided he can't wait till tomorrow for those dues. Be real insistent, get them both focused on him. There are two, right?"

Tyler nodded. "As far as we know."

"While he's doing that, Tony, you and me come down the stairs and get into the house. We find my mother and get her back up to the attic with us, then out over the roof before Tyler lets up on them."

"What if I can't keep their attention long enough?" Tyler asked. "Or they don't both come to the door?"

"I'll help with that," Angelica said. "We'll manage."

* * * * *

Diane sat ramrod straight, her fingers interlaced in her lap, with her eyes cast deliberately down and watching, peripherally but with all her attention fixed, the door to the kitchen. Hammer-man stood just a few feet away, his back to her, looking through her gauzy curtains into the street. The smaller man had parked himself by the door where Tyler had come knocking.

She had heard him, of course, knew what he was up to,

Exile 165

and wanted to call out to him but did not dare. Not to call for help—to tell him to run.

Her inner eyes were going crazy. Flashing scenes at her with the regularity of blinking—flashing in and out of the world where she sat. Living room. Darkness. Living room. Blood. Living room. Demon. Living room . . .

Her heart beat hard and fast, pushing panic through her veins. She stiffened her whole body against it.

She was trying to pray.

Her hands shook, and she tightened her fingers.

Diane had never learned to pray. It was a skill, something to be trained in, and she had resisted. Had refused to learn, in fact. Prayer was a full entering in. It was a flinging wide, a plunge, a total surrender to Oneness, bringing the Spirit surging and then riding the wave like a surfer racing toward shore. One with the wave, the exhilaration, the spray; One with the very ocean.

Some were better at it than others. But the abandonment that was true prayer never left anyone unchanged, and Diane had spent twenty years fighting to remain the same.

But now was different. Now was abandon yourself or lose everything. You gave everything when you surrendered to the Spirit, but you gave it to power, and sometimes the power turned and worked in your favour. That power was the only thing that could help her now. So she tried, desperately, to grasp the images flashing before her eyes and gather them into something coherent she could hold in her heart and offer—as a question, a request, an open door, a gap in the seawall to let the wave through.

Instead, panic kept balling up in her throat, and her racing heart made focus impossible.

The spirit is willing, but the flesh is weak, she thought.

Finally willing.

After all these years.

Even if for no other reason than sheer, selfish self-preservation.

Hammer-man moved over a little and made a grunting noise to himself, perhaps responding to something he saw in the street. His partner in the kitchen bumped into the stove, rattling the burners. She could not fathom why they had come here. She had spent two decades making herself as irrelevant to them as possible. Two decades hiding from the Spirit and trying to make the Oneness pay. Keeping herself apart so the Oneness couldn't have her, couldn't access her gift, couldn't love her, couldn't consider themselves part of her. They didn't deserve anything else. Not after what had happened to Douglas.

Minutes ticked past, and the panic subsided somewhat as the images thinned and lessened. Memory took their place, scenes rehearsed a thousand angry, grieving times.

The world did not often take notice of the Oneness. Diane had told Chris as much—they were hidden in plain sight. Until something happened to bring the war out of the shadows. Then, hostile, vengeful, malicious, the devils—the slanderers—came boiling into the lives of human beings and tore into the Oneness with all the collected powers of human fear and demon hate.

The results took many forms. Twenty years ago it had taken the form of an out-and-out pogrom. Citing suspicion of cult activities, police had begun investigating a large Oneness cell. In the midst of that, the cell house was firebombed, killing men, women, and children. No one knew who was responsible for the bombing. A few people got out. Stragglers were chased—some by the police, some by demons, some by others who hounded them down and murdered them. There had been other factors in it all, witchcraft, possession. The police had not meant for things to get out of hand as they did. The enemy had engineered it all.

Mary's family were some of the few. The father and husband, Sam, had packed his wife and four children in a station wagon and just hit the road, driving as far and as fast as he could. Mary, his twin sister, accompanied them. They had nothing but the clothes on their backs, and when they ran out of gas, they left the car and started walking. Douglas found them on the side of the road and picked them up. He'd only intended to take them into town, get them to a phone or something so they could find help. Of course, he had no idea when he saw them walking single-file along the highway how much trouble they were in. Or how electrifying their presence would be.

Most of all, he hadn't expected their love. The children were just children—the same mix of precocious and shy that would be expected in most families. But Sam, his wife, and Mary— they were different. Something about the way they interacted, the way they spoke, the way their eyes met exposed something deep inside Diane's husband that undid him completely. He didn't drop them off somewhere. He brought them home and hid them.

At first Diane hadn't known what to think of them, but after they'd been in the house twenty minutes, she was as sucked in as Douglas was. Conversation happened, and that night over

Rachel Starr Thomson

multiple pots of coffee, their talk turned the world upside down and inside out. They were electric, magnetic, true. Especially Mary. From the moment Sam's twin sister walked into the house, Diane knew nothing would ever be the same. Mary wasn't just a new acquaintance, not just a potential friend. She was a promise of a life more real, more full and beautiful, than anything Diane had never known.

In the end it was Mary's fault, everything that had happened.

The police came looking for them, and Douglas lied and managed to turn them away. Sam and his wife wanted to leave. Others would come after them; they decided it was too dangerous to Douglas and Diane for them to stay. They should go find a place in the cliffs, hide away from people, and try to fight the demons off. Sam was certain that they were being followed. Douglas hated the idea—he'd already made the family his responsibility and had no intention of letting them go out from under his protection until it was safe. But Sam was as iron willed as Douglas, and he would have won if Mary hadn't talked him out of it.

That night she had convinced Sam that staying with the Sawyers was the right thing to do. That the Spirit had led them here, and here was where they should remain. She had convinced him that even if it cost something, it was the better thing to do. The woman had a tongue like silver. Even Diane believed her.

In fact, that night Diane crossed over. As Mary spoke of the Spirit and the world of the Oneness, Diane believed it—and as Mary held out her hand, Diane took it and became one of them.

Douglas did not. Mary had told Diane, with a twinkle in

her eye, that he wouldn't resist long. It was humbling to cross over—there was a surrender, an undoing of yourself to find yourself again as part of something bigger. It was hard for some to do. Especially a man as proud and self-sufficient as Diane Sawyer's husband.

They lived there two months. The Sawyer house functioned like a cell, with Diane learning that she had a gift of eyes and Sam teaching her about prayer and Mary teaching her about living connected. The world was transformed. Douglas admired his wife's new identity but wouldn't enter it with her. She turned her first prayers in the direction of his conversion.

But the demons came after all. They came human: inhabiting the bodies of three teenage boys, high as kites and crazed. They slaughtered the children and the couple and Douglas, who tried to fight them. He was the only one who fought. The Oneness refused to battle those boys. Douglas died trying to protect Mary, and then Mary held Diane back. Held her, with her small frame and her arms that were too strong for her size. She dragged her out of the house and forced her into hiding, and for some reason the demons didn't come looking for them.

Douglas took a few hours to die of his injuries. Diane sat with him and clutched his hand and cried and tried to talk to him, but his eyes were glassed over and he didn't say a word. She didn't know if he knew she was there. Her sharpest memory was the blood.

Mary stayed in the village after that, becoming the leader of a tiny cell. And Diane never, ever, ever forgave her. Her most bitter regret was crossing over. Her greatest fear was that Chris would follow her.

She had not actually thought to fear that the demons would come again. Mary's cell was so small it was laughable. And Diane kept herself out of it.

Her head came up sharply at a pounding on the front door. Hammer-man turned to face the kitchen but did not move. The smaller man answered the door and she heard Tyler's voice again, uncharacteristically pushy and argumentative. Diane would have laughed and admired their persistence if she hadn't been so afraid for him.

And then she heard movement behind the door at the base of the attic stairs.

They hadn't.

She couldn't stop her eyes from darting to Hammer-man. He looked stoic and unmoved as voices in the kitchen rose. Chris would be coming through that attic door any minute. Tyler was doing his best to create a distraction, but the huge guard wasn't budging.

She saw the shadow through the gauze curtains an instant before the window broke and flew in pieces into the room. Hammer-man whirled around just in time for a pair of feet to slam into his chest, knocking him backwards though not over. The intruder landed on the floor in a catlike crouch. It was a girl Diane had never seen before, though she knew immediately the girl was Oneness.

Hammer-man charged her, and she rolled out of the way and brought a heavy iron poker into the back of his knee. He roared in pain but still didn't fall. She ducked another charge. In the kitchen, Tyler had forced his way through the door and climbed half up the smaller man's back with his arm wrapped around the man's neck. He was shouting. So was the girl. And then someone else was there—a boy, strikingly like the girl in appearance and apparently trained to fight. He took Hammer-man down with a rapid series of blows, but the huge guard was up on his feet again in seconds. He pulled a gun.

And someone was at her feet, undoing the restraints that kept her in her chair. She twisted her head to see who it was. Chris. He had her feet loose and practically manhandled her out of the chair, big hands tight on her shoulders, and pushed her toward the attic door. "Get out," he said through gritted teeth.

The gun went off. Tyler and the smaller man were in the living room, still struggling; Hammer-man had the dark-haired boy by the collar; Diane's eyes were blurred with tears as she struggled to see who had been shot. Chris shoved her—hard—at the attic door.

"Get out!" he roared.

And it was the past all over again. One domino after another.

Into the confusion a thought came to her with crystal clarity: if Chris succeeded in saving her life, would she hate him for it like she hated Mary?

There was a little hollow under the thicket, and Richard and Mary and the hermit tucked themselves there, hiding under the bushes and watching as David's men searched the house and spilled back into the yard. Aware that they were close enough to be heard in the still air, they said nothing. Shadows were lengthening with early evening, and they hoped the patterns created by the light would help them melt into their surroundings.

They tensed as one man stood ten feet away and scanned the cliff. His eyes widened, and he turned on his heel and jogged toward the house.

"Caught," Richard whispered.

"Do we run?" Mary asked very quietly.

Too late. David strode up to the group, holstering a revolver as he did so. His greeting burst out, taking them all by surprise.

"Richard! Mary! Thank God you're all right!"

Richard steeled his voice. "What are you doing here, David?"

David stopped just short of being close enough for a handshake, halfway up the hill and standing at a definite disadvantage. His approach couldn't be less threatening. The other men waited just a little behind him.

"Looking for you, my friend," David said. "We got wind of trouble and have been searching for you everywhere. The Spirit led us here."

"Us?" Richard said, raising an eyebrow at the other men. "They aren't Oneness."

David flushed. "They're friends."

"You know what they are," the hermit growled.

"David," Richard said carefully, "do you know what these men are?" All four were standing in a line behind David, waiting, unassuming. They didn't look threatening. If anything, they seemed . . . blank.

"Do you have Reese with you?" David asked. "Some of my cell followed you to the warehouse—we were worried about your safety. They told me what happened there. That you found Reese."

"Why does that matter to you?" Mary asked.

David flushed and looked down, the picture of sorrow. "I had to exile her, Mary, you know that. That doesn't mean I took joy in it. She's obviously in trouble. If there's anything we can do to bring her back . . ."

"It's a little late for remorse in that direction, don't you think?" Richard asked. "What did you do when you originally exiled her, pack her into the street with nothing but the clothes on her back?"

David brought his eyes up and met Richard's gaze sharply. "We did all we could for her, but she didn't want our help. She was resistant."

Richard didn't let him keep going. "You're lying, David," he said. "Reese was never cut off from the Oneness. You had no authority to do what you did. No one can cut another off."

David looked genuinely confused. "What are you trying to say?"

"Honestly? I'm not sure. But something is very wrong. And you've lied. I'm not sure what to do with that."

Before he could respond, the hermit spoke.

"I know you!"

David turned, obviously surprised. "What?"

The old man pointed a shaky figure, squinting in David's face. "I know you. I remember you. You came here when you were just a young one. Just a few days after the bombing."

"You're mistaken," David said. "I've never been on this mountain, and I don't know you."

"You're lying again," the hermit said. He cocked his head as though he was trying to take in David's face from another angle, like that would prompt the memories out of sluggishness and back into play. "Yes, I remember. Those were terrible days. You lost too much in them." He raised his eyebrows. "You wanted to be cut loose."

"What?" Mary asked, turning to David. "What does he mean?"

The hermit carried on. "You wanted to be free of the Oneness. You came here to ask me to do it. But I couldn't—no one can. And you left here angry."

Richard's eyes opened wide, and he looked first at the men standing silently behind David and then back at the cell leader.

And he knew.

"The hive . . ." Richard said slowly. "You've been responsible for years to attack the hive, and you kept things on the defensive. Then Reese started hearing from the Spirit because you weren't doing your job. And you accused her of betraying her cell. You told her she'd been headstrong and independent and a fool, and that she'd caused the death of good people, and you told her she'd lost her place in the Oneness because of it. And you managed to project enough of yourself that you cloaked her—you're where the deception comes from. Reese isn't the exile. You are!"

"And why try so hard to protect the hive?" the hermit put in.

Once asked, the answer was clear—so solid, so apparent that it couldn't be denied.

Mary felt it like a blow. "The hive, David—it wasn't centred in that warehouse. It's centred in you."

With the words spoken and hanging in the air, the look of wounded confusion left David's face. Without hurrying, he unholstered the revolver at his waist and pointed it at Mary. "I think it's time you both stop talking," he said.

Mary's face went white, but her fear didn't dim her anger. "You can't bring your demonic forces in here!" she said. "This place is under a shield!"

David cocked the gun. "I don't need to," he said. "This isn't demonic, my dear. This is human."

"Why?" Mary asked.

"Reese was going to discover me," David said. "With her insistence on going after the hive. The Spirit was leading her straight to me. I had to get rid of her somehow, and the exile was better than a killing. It gave me power—it gave the core power. Power enough to finally, finally come after you."

"Me?" Mary said.

"You brought me into the Oneness," David said. "Twenty-three years ago. I don't think you even remember—that's how little you care." His grip on the gun tightened. "I want nothing more than to be rid of the Oneness. Since the Spirit won't set me free, I'll cut myself loose in my own way. Starting with you—all of you."

"You'll do what demons fear to do?" Mary asked quietly.

He waited.

She glared at him. "I don't know where April is, but I'm sure now you're responsible for her disappearance. Whoever took her, they didn't kill her. Afraid to shed blood. Now you'll do what demons are afraid of? David, reconsider. You said yourself you can't be free of the Spirit. I hate to think what blood on your hands—Oneness blood—will mean for you."

"Blood," David spat. "You think I'm afraid of a little blood? I didn't know the meaning of the word until the Oneness forced me to it. Death cannot come quickly enough for me. And I cannot be any more damned than I am while I'm still a part of all of you!"

Before anyone saw it coming, Richard stepped forward and

put his hand on the revolver, gently but firmly bearing it down. "What happened to your family twenty years ago was not the Oneness's doing. You know that. It was the enemy who inspired that attack."

"What do you know about it? You weren't there!"

"Mary has told me about the bombing and the massacre," Richard said. "You're not the only one who lost everything—the only one who needs healing . . ."

"I know where to find healing," David said. Richard's grip had grown tight, both on the revolver and on David's hand. The cell leader relaxed his arm for a moment and then unexpectedly brought it up, twisting free of Richard's grip and clubbing him across the face with the gun. Blood gushed from Richard's nose, and he staggered backwards with David still beating the gun around his head and shoulders, wild and uncontrolled. Mary grabbed the cell leader's other arm and held it, trying unsuccessfully to drag him away from Richard.

"David," she screamed as the men with him came charging up the hill to intervene. "Stop it! Stop it, you can't do this!"

One of the men grabbed her and threw her off, and she fell to the ground. Richard lurched back as David straightened up and glared at them. "Don't you tell me what I can't do."

Mary struggled back to her feet, holding her abdomen as though someone had kicked it. "David, how are you doing this? How can you deny the connection—the Spirit? Everyone else?"

"I can't," he growled, and his voice slowly slid back to normal. It was steely now, dreadfully controlled. "No matter how hard I try, no matter how badly I want to, I can't leave the Oneness. So I will make the Oneness leave me."

"You know it wasn't our fault," Mary said, still crouching in the dirt. The hermit laid a hand on her shoulder, but Mary's eyes didn't leave David. "We didn't cause the massacre. That was the demons—the creatures you've sided with. You've become what you hate, David."

"No," he countered. "What I hate is you. All these years the demonic has been offering us freedom. A return to primal chaos, freedom from the Spirit holding—binding—this world together. Freedom from each other. I want that freedom, Mary. It's my choice, and I'm choosing it."

"And everyone else along with you?" the hermit said. "You can't just make a choice like that for yourself. If you succeeded you'd be taking away everyone else's right to choose."

"I don't care," David said. He looked down at the gun still in his hand, smiled, and shot the old man.

Mary screamed out as the hermit dropped in the dust, blood soaking the hand he held against his abdomen. David holstered the revolver and nodded to his cohorts. "Tie those two up and get them in the car. We're going to do this thing right."

"What do you mean?" Mary found the voice to ask.

His eyes glimmered. "I'm not going to kill you out here, under a shield where the effort would be half-wasted. I'm going to kill you where it counts."

Mary's stomach sank, and she knew what he was going to say before he finished.

"We're going back to the warehouse."

Bound hand and foot so tightly that they could not move, the companions were laid side by side in the back of the station wagon and covered with a thick blanket. It was damp and musty and smelled like old gasoline and grease, and the air beneath the blanket turned quickly heavy and suffocating.

They were silent as the car started and pulled away from the hermitage.

Outside, it was growing darker.

"Reese," Mary whispered.

* * * * *

Reese tried her valiant best to lift April and carry her out of the cave before giving up. Her efforts only served to make it clear how weak she actually was from the attack. Straightening up, an attack of nausea nearly knocked her off balance, weariness sweeping through her core and every limb. She sat for a moment, letting her legs regain their strength. All around her, the painting told its terrible story. And April slept.

"Listen," Reese said, peering down at her unconscious companion, "you hang on. I'm going to get Mary and Richard, and they'll get you out of here as soon as they can. You only have to hang in there for a little while longer. Okay? Just an hour, and we'll have you out."

She looked up, the scenes glimmering in the torchlight. The little village cell was there, and Chris and Tyler. The woman she had seen on the path and in the cave had been drawn in especially vivid detail, even the compassion in her eyes showing. She swallowed hard at the images of herself, of the hive, of the hive's secret. Her mouth set in a grim line.

"And we'll make sure this story finishes well," she heard herself say.

Sore, she stood and put the torch out in the wet earth around the edges of the cave. The light outside temporarily blinded her as she emerged, the low evening sun shining directly into her eyes. Leaving April behind went against all her instincts, but she reasoned that the girl had been left to die; no one was likely to come after her now, and she was better off sheltered in the cave than being carried or dragged by Reese, who would likely collapse if she tried it. She wasn't happy with her own weakness, but going back to Richard and Mary was the best thing she could do.

She wondered if they were still arguing with the hermit. Maybe so, she told herself. It doesn't matter. You know the truth now.

Knew it, but could not feel it. She felt as exiled as she had when she entered the cave. The only new emotion—rising and growing the longer the painting lingered in her mind—was anger. Outrage, even, carrying with it a blinding new hurt but acting as its own defence against that hurt. She had not been exiled by the Spirit; she had never been in the wrong. She had been targeted—mercilessly and maliciously targeted by one she had trusted.

Deliberately, she ducked the boiling emotion by turning her thoughts back to April. As her eyes adjusted to the light, she pushed herself back up the path toward the hermit's house.

She was close enough to hear when the gun went off. Running was her first response, her automatic reaction, but her feet slipped on the sandy path—or just gave up placing themselves properly—and she went down. As she did, she felt the bleeding wound in her side tear and gape further. She rolled over and stared. Blood was spreading across her abdomen, staining her hands. She had already stained the ground where she had fallen.

Suddenly scared, she pushed herself up and forced her legs to work again, to carry her toward the hermit. She heard Mary's scream and the sounds of a fight. The cliffs were blurring on every side. No, no, no. Not now. She couldn't pass out now. She had to make it back in time to help . . .

Her legs refused to keep holding her up, and she crawled forward, one hand clutching her side, blood soaking her sleeve and dripping to the ground beneath her. She gritted her teeth and crawled up over a ridge, just in time to see the station wagon pull away.

David. He'd found them.

Shivering, and then convulsing, she dragged herself another three feet toward a hollow in the cliff and then fell forward.

Letting out a long groan, she realized she wasn't alone.

The hermit was there.

He was staring at her.

He was dead. Wasn't he?

He wasn't . . . he moved. His hand inched up toward her face.

She licked her lips, wanting to tell him the truth.

"Forgive me," he whispered.

His eyes still stared like a dead man's; she wasn't even sure he could see her. But he knew she was there. She tried to answer him but couldn't. Her voice too was bleeding out into the sandy ground.

"I was wrong," he went on. "You were cloaked . . . I was wrong. I should have helped you. Forgive me."

One of them moved—she wasn't sure who—close enough that the hermit's hand could reach her. He laid it on her forehead and whispered something in a language she did not know— Spirit tongue, Spirit words. As he spoke them, something inside her fluttered to life, and a warmth began to spread throughout her body.

"I am . . . a healer," he told her. "The Spirit brought you to me to be healed. I'm sorry."

She got the words out seconds before he breathed his last. "I forgive you."

On her back, she gazed up at the sky. It was intensely blue— hardly a cloud—and the tops of pine trees and the sandy sweep of ridges rimmed it. The sun slanted down, its rays softening as the day drew to a close. She lay next to a dead man and mulled over his words as the warmth spread and pulsed through her—a miracle, she thought. She ought to be dead as he was. She ought to be bleeding to death. But the bleeding had stopped. And she was getting stronger.

The last act of mercy by the hermit of Tempter's Mountain was doing its work. And a good thing, too, she thought. No one else knew where April was. No one else knew that David had taken Richard and Mary. And no one else knew the truth about the hive, about the betrayal—

She still felt herself to be an exile, but as she gained strength and stared into the sky, Reese knew it didn't matter. There was work to be done, and she was the only one who could do it.

Exile

Maybe it was his growing habit of trying to imagine the world from a Oneness perspective. Or maybe stress was just causing him to see things. Either way, Tyler was growing more aware by the minute of a world more buzzingly alive, both more glorious and more menacing, than he had ever before imagined.

"Kecak," Hammer-man answered his cell phone. "Yeah, we got them."

Tyler heard the voice on the other end say something, but he couldn't make out words. Just another thug taking orders from another crime boss, like he'd seen a million times on TV as a kid. Not that Tyler had ever expected to get mixed up in the world of organized crime, but guns and abductions and thugs with cell phones were about as grittily real-world as you could get.

Except that he was pretty sure both these men were demon possessed, and he could still see Patrick watching.

It was a weird world Reese had pulled him into.

Beside him, leaning against the wall inside Diane's kitchen, Tony was as white as a proverbial ghost. (Real ghosts, if Patrick was anything like representative, were not pale at all.) He sat with his jaw locked against the pain of the bullet lodged just above his knee, and he was sweating. Angelica sat beside him looking nearly as pale as her twin. All three were trussed hand and foot with plastic zip ties. Chris and Diane sat across from them, leaning against the stove, and the tattooed man stalked between the rows, glowering down at them and brandishing an obvious gun. Angelica glared back at him. Tyler did not. He had once earlier—looked into the man's eyes. He saw something inhuman there, a presence darting around behind the man's face, and it shook him so badly he kept his eyes down.

Can't you do something? he wondered in Patrick's direction, asking himself at the same time whether ghosts could really be expected to read minds. Maybe they could if you were Oneness. Patrick was standing in the window, feet on the sill, head bent because he was too tall to fit in there, but he did nothing. The dimming light of dusk made him seem even more a shadow than usual.

Hammer-man clipped his cell phone shut. "Let's get 'em in the car. We're going to the warehouse."

Tattoos grinned ghoulishly. He grabbed Angelica's arm and hauled her to her feet. Her ankles were tied too closely together to keep her balanced, but he kept her from falling. "Open the trunk."

They had pulled their car up so it was only feet from the kitchen door, tucked behind the house where neighbours wouldn't see. Hammer-man obeyed, shoving a few things out of the way. As he pulled his head back up from the depths of the trunk, he paused and scanned the sky. "You hear anything?"

Tattoos frowned. "No."

"Listen!" the bigger thug insisted.

Dumping Angelica into the trunk, Tattoos paused. "Sounds like demons."

"So no problem, right?" Hammer-man said. But he sounded nervous.

Both men picked up their pace, and Tyler found himself grabbed and shoved headfirst into the trunk, falling on his shoulder and landing with his feet in Angelica's face.

"Sorry," he said.

"Shh," she shot back. "Listen."

Tony was dumped in after them, moaning with the pain and temporarily distracting both twins. Hammer-man slammed the trunk shut.

But Tyler was listening now.

He heard it at first like a high-up, far-off screech, growing louder like a plane diving or a bomb dropping. Then the sound grew to a roar, both thugs were cursing and someone else—someone new—was shouting something. Car doors slammed and the car roared to life, grinding gravel under its tires. All three occupants of the trunk slammed into the car frame and each other.

"Hang in there, Tony," Angelica said.

But Tyler was exulting.

Whatever had just happened, they had left Diane and Chris behind.

And the voice he had heard unmistakably belonged to Reese.

* * * * *

On the road in the old hermit's Chevy truck, Reese had pushed the speed limit as far as she could without risking being pulled over. As soon as she reached the village, she headed straight for the harbour, parked at the main marina, and strode up the central street toward Diane's. As she went, she deliberately loosed every emotion, every crippling cry of her soul: her anger, her grief, her horrifying sense of being alone. She kept her eyes fixed on the street that rose up the hill before her, willing her hands to stay unclenched and her spirit to stay open.

Why?

Why me? Why would you do this to me? How could you all look the other way—how could you buy into the lie? Don't you know how badly I've hurt?

Tears blinded her, but she kept going, kept her heart open, let the questions turn into blind, twisting pain.

She had been a target from the moment she first stepped foot in this village—a magnet for every spiteful renegade and foolhardy devil in this place. And because proximity was power, they would only get bolder as she drew nearer to the hive members in Diane's house.

The high-off screech began half a block from the Sawyer house, and she broke into a run, praying that God himself would time this. April's painting had pointed her this far, but once she got there, she was on her own.

No, something deep within corrected her. Never on your own.

Diane Sawyer's house was just above the road on a three-foot bluff; Reese leaped up, ran for the front-door step, and finally dared to look back.

Her eyes widened. Six. Six demon creatures in bird bodies were hurtling straight at her.

Perfect.

Instead of calling the sword to her hand and meeting the attack head-on, Reese flung the front door open and hit the floor, sending the creatures shooting over her head and slamming into the tattooed man who was pulling Diane to her feet in a direct line from the front door. He went down, firing his gun and cursing. Two of the demons had gone even further, flying over the tattooed man's head, and crashed headlong into the other thug, who was standing outside behind a black car.

"Damn it!" the big man shouted. "Kelly, get in the car!"

Kelly, the tattooed man, swung his revolver and hit one of the creatures in the head, and the demon turned on him, pecking and beating at his head and shoulders. It had effectively beaten him away from Diane, who was, Reese realized, startled, free—the zip ties around her wrists and ankles had been cut.

Still lying flat on the floor, she looked to Chris. He was on his feet with a penknife in his hand.

Good man, she thought.

They didn't have much time before the creatures figured out they were battling each other. She prayed again for timing.

And it worked. The men were gone, both of them jumping

Exile   189

into the car and hitting the gas. "Run hard!" she shouted. "I'm coming after you!"

Closing her hand, she felt the sword taking shape even as the bird creatures turned their eyes in the direction of her shout. "That's right," she said quietly as the blade in her hand became solid and hot. "Come and get me."

Three of them rushed her at once, but they were hindered by the tight space, and Reese took them two and then one, dispatched in quick strokes. The tattooed man had put a bullet through one, momentarily slowing it down, and it wasn't hard to kill as it launched itself at her with a snarl. The last two hung back, eyes glowing, glaring at her with a hatred that sent a shiver down her spine.

Yet somehow, it felt good to be hated.

Chris turned her direction, went pale, and shouted, "Look out!"

Claws hooked into her shoulders from behind, and a heavy weight bore her to the floor. She'd lost. With the other two just waiting for her to slip, there was no coming back from this one . . .

But she heard a shriek, and the weight on her back ripped off and back; she made it to her feet again just in time to dispatch the two remaining demons that were coming in for the kill.

Panting, unbelieving, she whirled around to see the dead body of the attacker from behind, curling and shrivelling back to its bird form. It had been decapitated. Not by her.

She turned back. Three feet away, Diane was standing with a sword glowing in her hand, staring at the dead bird.

Reese nodded, her eyes filling with tears. "Thank you."

Diane couldn't seem to find a voice, but she nodded in response.

Chris gave his mother a hard stare and then turned back to Reese. "They got away with the others. We have to go after them."

"We will," Reese told him. "I know where they've gone." Without an enemy to fight, her sword was fading away, and she relaxed her grip and let it go. Diane followed suit. Reese rested her hand on Diane's shoulder. "And this time we're going to win."

Diane jerked herself away. "There's no we."

Chris shook his head and stuffed his hands in his pockets. "Tyler's out there, Mum. You can't fight this right now."

She turned on him. "What do you know about it? Your father—"

"Died, if I had to guess, fighting for something he believed in," Chris shot back. "When did you decide that staying out of the fight was the best way to honour him?"

To both their surprise, Diane started to cry. "The Oneness—it's supposed to be this idyllic, this wonderful thing . . . this thing that changes your life for the better. And all it does is bring loss and pain and hardness."

"No," Reese said. "The Oneness is no idyll. Nobody knows that more than I do. From the day I became One, I've learned to fight and to strive and to endure. The Oneness opens your eyes to the darkness. But the darkness is real, Diane—trying to hide from it doesn't change that." Her voice softened, and she placed her hand on Diane's shoulder again, a touch as loving as a daughter's and just as sincere. "But it's not all there is. The wonder is real, too, and the light—and the love. But you won't know it if you don't choose to walk in it. To endure even when things are hard."

The older woman broke down. Shaking, sobbing, she clung to Reese and vented twenty years of grief on the girl's shoulder.

And Reese, who still could not feel the truth of what she believed, chose to believe the truth of her own words, and she comforted Diane with all the compassion she could find within her.

Chris turned away and waited in stony silence until his mother's sobs wore thin. "We have to go," he said finally.

"We know," Reese said. "We're coming."

"I'm going with you."

"Of course you are."

"Don't you want me to convert first?" Chris whirled around and stared hard at her.

She looked unflinchingly back at him. "Of course I do."

He swallowed. "Blast it, girl. It isn't fair, what I feel about you."

Her voice dropped to a near whisper. "I know. But Oneness is first."

Diane looked between the two of them and shook her head. "You two are not choosing an easy path."

Reese, her arm still around the older woman, looked at Diane and smiled. "Right now I don't think we're choosing

"So how are we going to do this? Last time you went in there you just about got slaughtered."

Between the looks Chris kept giving her, apparently examining her to make sure she actually was healed from the last attack, Reese told him and Diane everything she had learned about the hive and David's treachery. Chris's assertion that the thugs were heading for the warehouse only confirmed what she already knew.

Opening the door to Chris's truck and swinging herself in, she ducked her eyes when she caught Chris staring at her again.

"What?"

"I don't understand why that hermit didn't heal you right away."

Reese flushed. "He thought . . . he thought wrong things. About me. You know that."

"Mary and Richard weren't so sure about you either, for

a while. You're putting your neck on the line for people who couldn't decide until yesterday whether you were the enemy or not."

"I'm putting my neck on the line for the Oneness, Chris. My family. You would do the same."

"If I was one of you."

"Which, unfortunately, you're not."

They stared at each other, locking into one another's eyes for a long moment. Reese looked away first. Diane was standing beside the truck. Behind her, her house was full of light—she had turned every lamp and lightbulb on after the dead birds were cleared out, trying to restore some sense of homeliness and security. It was dark outside, and the lights blazed out with warmth.

"Are you coming?" Reese asked.

Diane looked at her son as though pleading for help.

"For Tyler," he said.

"No," Reese said, shaking her head. "No. For Mary. And Richard. And April. Your cell, your family. For the world. For the Oneness."

She met Diane's eyes without flinching. "For me."

"I wish I was more like you," Diane said. "But I'm not."

Reese nodded slowly. "Okay." She turned to Chris. "We need to go. I don't know how much time we have left, but I don't think it's much."

He turned the ignition and the truck roared to life. Reese put her hand on Chris's arm. "You don't have to come," she said.

"You know I'm not going to stay behind."

"I'm not sure we're going to win this one. Not without your mother."

"How much help can she be? She's never even carried one of those sword things before today."

"It isn't about that. It's about the Oneness—everyone joined together, everyone being who and what they are. She is one of us. We need her. If she won't see that . . . I just don't know what's going to happen out there, Chris."

He set his jaw and backed the truck out of the driveway. "We're going to get Tyler out of there, that's what we're going to do. And the rest of them."

Reese nodded, but she was staring out the window now, bleakly taking in the village street and the shadowy view of the bay passing by. The hour's drive to Lincoln passed in tense, unhappy silence. When they were ten miles from the exit, Reese started talking.

"We'll go in from above. There's a fire exit from an upstairs catwalk down to the ground outside. Once we get in, we'll have to find out what's going on—where they are, what exactly they're doing. I need you to be the one to do that."

"So the demons don't get you."

"Something like that, yes. If the fight starts too soon, we won't have time to free the others."

"Tell me again why we aren't calling in the Lincoln cell."

Reese shook her head. "They won't be ready to believe me against David. That will come, but . . . not yet. And I wouldn't want them to. Loyalty is a hard thing to change."

Chris cast her a curious look, keeping his eyes mostly on the road. "Does it hurt you? Fighting him?"

"He's still one of us."

"Like my mother."

"A little bit."

Her voice grew quiet with every answer, like the words took too much effort and caused pain.

"I'm sorry she wouldn't come."

Reese smiled. "It's not your fault."

"She's angry . . . still. She blames all of you for my father's death."

"Anger is dangerous."

"So is grief."

Reese half-turned so that she was facing Chris, who kept looking straight ahead. "What do you mean by that?"

"You're still grieving this whole exile thing. You've been swallowed by it since we found you. I don't know why you haven't been able to cut loose, but if you don't, I think it's going to drown you. Maybe at a really bad time."

She glanced down at her hands. "I don't know how to cut loose. I believe what Richard and Tyler said . . . I know they're right. I saw it in April's painting. But I can't feel it. I still feel what it felt like to be cut off . . . to be cast out. To be treated like an enemy by everyone I love."

"I can't imagine," Chris said honestly. "But you can't go into the warehouse weighed under by all that. If you do, you're not going to make it back out."

She considered his words. "You might be right."

"I am."

"What makes you such an expert in grief?" Reese winced. "I'm sorry. I know better . . . your father . . ."

"Nope," Chris said. "I was too young. Don't even remember him. That's why I didn't remember any of this Oneness business from all those years ago either. Yeah, I've missed having him around, but it isn't like losing someone I'd learned to love."

"Then what does make you such an expert?" Reese asked, gently teasing but genuinely curious at the same time.

"Tyler."

"Tyler?"

"Tyler's parents died when he was ten. He was an only child—totally alone in the world after that. It wasn't just a death; it was like the end of the world. It tore his whole universe apart. He took years to get to some sense of normal—some kind of sense of functional and whole. Mum and I did all we could for him, but still . . . years."

He flicked his eyes off the road and drilled them into her. "Reese, you do not have years."

She looked out the window. "Exit's coming up."

He ignored her. "If Tyler dies tonight it's going to be the end of my world. But I don't want to lose you either."

She smiled faintly. "I understand."

He pulled off at the exit. "I hope you do."

* * * * *

Mary stood in the centre of the warehouse floor, arms folded and eyes angry. Richard was stretched out on the ground beside her. His body lay facedown, but his head was turned so that Tyler could see how battered his face looked—one eye was swollen shut, and his nose was purple. His face was heavily streaked with blood. No one seemed to be guarding them, but Mary's rigidity suggested otherwise.

Oh. Demons.

Right.

So much for Reese teaming up with the village cell.

The thugs pulled the twins out of the car and dumped Tony roughly on the ground, then reached down to cut the zip tie around Angelica's ankles so she could walk to the warehouse. The moment they did, she erupted into a kicking, biting tornado, calling heaven down on them both in Italian. Kelly backhanded her across the warehouse, and Tyler found himself suddenly boiling over. When Hammer-man cut the tie around his ankles, it was all he could do not to follow Angelica's example.

Save it, he told himself. You can grandstand when they try to kill you.

He got to his feet, and Hammer-man prodded him toward Mary. Angelica walked beside him, holding the back of one hand to her cheek, muttering something. Kelly's gun was in her shoulder, or she would have turned to get Tony. As it was, her brother was left lying on the asphalt.

Tyler felt the moment they passed through the demonic guard. The air around turned darker for half a second, and his hair stood on end. Mary was watching him with an expression that told him she could see everything. It was mingled with another expression altogether—tenderness. Compassion.

His mother would have been her age.

One more time, he pretended he was Oneness. This was his mother he was walking toward. He crossed the warehouse beside his sister. Richard, on the ground, a father—the best kind of father, one who deserved to be looked up to.

And then he stopped pretending.

All at once, they were his family, and he was home.

He was Oneness. He saw it again—the grid, the threads running through everything, connecting it all, the layers and layers of meaning and purpose. His spirit swelled and encompassed the universe, touched a million hearts, contracted back down to his own body but brought it all along.

Mary looked at him and smiled slowly, and he heard her voice in his mind. Welcome, Tyler. Angelica turned startled eyes on him, but in her eyes too there was nothing but welcome.

And it was enough.

He lacked nothing.

He was marching to his death, and he was absurdly happy.

* * * * *

Chris parked the truck two warehouses away, over a chain-link fence and across two parking lots from the one they were targeting. They were in a hurry, but there was no sense in giving away their presence too soon. He and Reese got out and crossed the distance at a slow run, keeping to the shadows. It was a

Saturday night, close to eleven o'clock, but a few of the yards were lit and some even showed signs of activity.

"Should we alert someone? Ask for help?" Chris said in a low voice.

"No."

"Because . . ."

"Because we are going to deal with demons and no one here stands a chance. If any of them are vulnerable to possession we'd just end up with more enemies to fight."

"Oh." He hesitated, pausing mid-jog in front of the chain-link fence. "Am I vulnerable to possession?"

"Not right now."

"Why not?"

"Demons can't just come in. They need permission." She smiled wanly. "You're not exactly ripe for giving it."

He nodded uncertainly. "Good."

"You don't have to come," she said abruptly. "There may not be much you can do."

"Some of those people in there are just people. With human bodies. I can land a few punches. Or bullets. You handle the spiritual side."

They crossed the fence through a gap in the chain link and stood in the parking lot in back of the warehouse. Industrial lights glared lines across the asphalt, allowing them to see. The fire escape, slightly rusted but solid, wasn't more than fifty feet away.

"Deep breath," Chris said, staring at the massive tin building.

"Do you think we're in time?"

"We have to be," Reese said, her voice very small. "Come on."

* * * * *

Hammer-man and Kelly laid Tony out next to Richard. Both were breathing but thoroughly unconscious, which Tyler still thought was a good thing. He and Angelica stood on either side of Mary, both towering over the smaller woman.

He had never felt so proud to stand with anyone.

To die with anyone.

His thoughts were all over the place, and ridiculously light, which made him feel foolish. The Oneness had expanded him, and he was surprised at the peace that came with it. When he drew close to Mary he realized he knew her, to an extent he had never known anyone; he knew the integrity of her spirit, the gentleness, the depth of her leadership. He sensed the sadness in her past and the love that made her strong despite it. The others too; if he concentrated just a little, it was like parts of them crossed into him, forming bonds of mutual trust and understanding instantly. It made him happier than he had ever been, but he was going to die, and in that one reality he grew sad again—he would have liked much longer to know what it was to be Oneness.

But then he remembered Patrick, whose experience of Oneness had apparently not been cut off by death. He might just have a long time after all.

Was he grinning?

Apparently yes, as David stepped out of the shadows and snapped, "Stop smiling! What's wrong with you?"

The man's sharp eyes appraised Tyler in an instant, and his expression turned to disgust. "Oh. Well, let me spare you the disappointment. It wears off. And all you have left is the bondage."

"Love is not bondage, David," Mary said.

"Not until you don't want it." He stepped back and regarded her with interest. "You're where it all began for me. A twenty-year journey of regret."

"It's not too late for you," Mary said. "Even now, it's not too late. Let go of the bitterness—come back to us."

"I never left you," he said, his voice raw and caustic. "That is the problem."

He held out his hand, and one of his flunkies placed a gun in it. Tyler scanned the men who stood all around—braver now than he had been before, more able to face the reality of other beings behind their eyes. He could see the demons lurking there and sense their conflicted emotions—hunger, eagerness, and fear.

Fear?

David cocked the gun. "This was all supposed to happen sooner," he said. "We've needed more power. What I did to Patrick and Reese can only carry us so far. The demons were supposed to kill that girl of yours, and you were supposed to find her dead and come running to me for help, and I was supposed to kill you precisely here. I should have known better than to let demons handle it—they didn't want her blood on their hands. But I have you where I wanted you in the end. You'll die here and give more strength to the core, and I'll keep expanding the hive until it rivals the Oneness in its size, and then we will destroy you all. They can't do it on their own—they're too stupid and too scattered. But with me leading them, they're learning to operate as one."

"You're insane," Mary said.

"You told me that."

"You'll destroy the world."

"That is the point."

Mary stepped forward. Tyler and Angelica tensed, both ready to spring to her aid—not that they could do any good. She held her hand out. "David, come home."

"I'm going to kill you," he said. "I'm only sorry we can't make it more of a ceremony. But I'm in a hurry—and we have witnesses."

In the shadows all around, eyes began to appear, glimmering, leering at them. Bodiless eyes that made Tyler shiver. The sense of their presence—presences—grew. There were dozens. A hundred. Hundreds. Eager and afraid to witness the death of these who were Oneness.

The sound of a gunshot echoed through the warehouse, ringing off the tin walls and roof. David stared at the gun in his hand in momentary surprise.

Behind him, Hammer-man dropped.

Tyler wasn't exactly sure where the impulse came from, but he and Angelica sprang forward in exactly the same moment, simultaneously tackling David. Tyler barrelled into the man's chest and wrapped his arms around him while Angelica threw her weight against his ankles. He fell. Tyler tried to reach for the gun without letting go of David's arms, but the man was too strong. Angelica kicked the revolver out of his hand just before he burst free of Tyler's grip, turned and got on his knees, and landed a solid punch to Tyler's gut. Tyler curled up involuntarily, gasping for air while willing himself to get back on his feet. David scrambled back up and ducked a roundhouse kick from Angelica. Another gunshot from somewhere in the warehouse dropped Kelly. Mary was standing over Richard and Tony in a protective crouch. Two of David's goons rushed her, and Tyler watched in fascinated horror as she drove her sword into one, then the other. Shrieks burst out of both men, and they crumpled to the floor and writhed as a dark cloud leaked from their mouths and noses—dispossessed.

There were still two more. Tyler managed to get in two good breaths of air and get back to his feet. He balled his fists and went after the first one, hoping to rush the man before he could draw a gun. Angelica was still keeping David busy. Another shot—from above?—dropped the third one, but Tyler's target met his rush with a blow to the face, and Tyler was on the floor again, sure that his entire right eye had just caved in. He couldn't see—blood in his eyes or fainting, he wasn't sure which was blurring his vision. His legs were going like a dog chasing its tail in his sleep, but he was still on the ground, an easy target.

He felt something in his hand.

He couldn't see, and the pain splitting through his head was distracting, but there was something in his hand. It was hard and hot and pulsing—and in a moment he realized what it was.

A hilt.

A sword.

It came with a burst of inspiration. Still mostly blind, he drove it straight up just as the thug appeared over him. The blade went deep into the man's chest, and an ear-splitting shriek—a wail of shock, of anger, half-human and half-demon—emitted from his mouth. The rush of dark cloud from the man's mouth and nose smelled of sulphur, and his body twisted and shook. Tyler pulled his sword back in horror, his vision clearing just enough to see—much to his relief—that the blade had left no wound in the man's chest. There was no blood, no laceration—not even his clothes were torn. He would recover.

A phrase popped into his mind. The weapons of our warfare are not carnal.

He wasn't entirely sure what that meant.

Mary was still standing over the unconscious men. Angelica was standing in a defensive posture in front of them. David had backed away, half into the shadows. The thugs were down—

But the warehouse was far from emptied of threats.

All around, a growing stench thickened the air. The eyes were back—and beginning to grow faces and bodies around them. A high-pitched sound filled the warehouse, rattling the tin.

David laughed.

From behind, someone grabbed Tyler. He was about to throw a wild punch when he realized it was Chris, engulfing him in a bear hug. The next moment Chris shoved him away.

"Glad you're alive," he said.

"Thanks for coming," Tyler answered. Chris had a gun.

The source of the shots. He cocked it and pointed it at David. Angelica had picked up the rebel's gun after she kicked it away, and she too pointed the muzzle at David.

"We're not both going to miss," Chris said. "I already dropped your men. Now call your demons off."

"You seem to forget who's outnumbered here," David said.

"Yeah, but your goon squad won't bleed. You will. Call them off."

"I'm not sure I can," David said. His tone spoke great enjoyment. "You've made them hungry with all your killing."

Chris didn't flinch. "I did what I had to do."

"You'll notice your companions haven't killed anyone," David said. "For good reason. They know the price of blood. All you've done is hand yourself over to the darkness, my young friend. And whether or not you kill me, they are going to tear you to pieces. Just a word from me, and I win no matter what you do."

Beside him, Angelica faltered in her aim, but Chris held steady. "You're bluffing. You can't afford to die—you said it yourself. These creatures won't hold together without your leadership. You die here, your whole plan fails."

David took a step forward, into a strip of light falling from a lightbulb overhead. "You'll be killing one of the Oneness. Do you have any idea of the consequences of that act?"

Chris sniffed. "Someone's got to do it. You don't deserve to live, Oneness or not."

"Chris . . ." Mary said from behind him, warning.

"Don't you take his side!"

"Go ahead," David said, taking another step forward. "Look me in the eye and shoot me in cold blood. You're not sniping the enemy from above this time, boy. You're shooting an unarmed man who is ten feet away from you." He stepped forward again and stopped with his arms folded smugly across his chest. "And for what? For killing someone? No, I didn't do that—the only killer in here is you. For trifling with some girl's emotions? Maybe the demons won't tear you apart. Maybe they'll let you be found with a gun in your hand and everyone else in here dead. You'll go to prison for the rest of your life, however long that may be. You can try all you want to tell the police that you were only trying to combat a warehouse full of demons, but I don't think it will help you much. Shame to bring so much embarrassment to your mother. Who, I notice, is not here."

Chris stared hard at him, the gun still steady, both hands clamped around it.

"Listen, kid, take a page from her book and look out for your own best interest. You can't save the day here. You can save yourself. I don't have any quarrel with you. You've been smart enough to keep yourself out of the Oneness. Now be smart enough to get yourself out of their business."

Chris pulled the trigger.

Nothing happened.

The gun was empty.

David laughed, a slow chuckle that built up to a guffaw. On every side, demon bodies took ephemeral shape. Chris slowly lowered the gun.

"Chris, get out of here," Tyler heard himself saying. "I don't think they care about you."

Mary spoke calmly but loudly enough for everyone to hear. "It's good advice. Take it, Chris. The rest of you take it too. We can't win this fight—there are too many. But we might be able to run. The farther we get from this warehouse, the weaker they'll get." She nodded toward the goons Chris had dropped. "They've got car keys—we get them, we get outside, and we drive away as fast as we can. Understand? That's the whole strategy. Run."

"Do we split up?" Tyler asked. He could feel pressure growing in his hand again, and the sword took shape as he spoke. A longer, more deadly looking blade had already formed itself in Angelica's hand.

"No," Mary said. "Keep together. Our strength is in Oneness."

Slowly, a laugh began to sound in the warehouse. It grew, hundreds of voices joining together, until the horde of demons mocked their intentions with a single voice.

Mary crouched low, her sword ready. "Now."

When they were boys and Tyler was still battling grief and all the demons grief brought with it, Chris had made up a game. It was called "Berzerker." The boys would go outside with their stick swords and pretend they were heroes being attacked by a gigantic army. And they would both swing their swords and howl and scream and leap around like maniacs and just fight and fight and fight and fight until Tyler found relief in exhaustion. Tyler didn't realize until much later how much wisdom Chris had shown in making up that game. Maybe even Chris hadn't known what he was doing—after all, he was only twelve when Tyler lost his parents.

But one thing Tyler learned from that game was that fighting was not actually all that complicated. The carefully choreographed routines in the movies were misleading. Talk of wartime strategy was inspiring but not all that useful in a backyard game of Berzerker. Real fighting was just a matter of swinging and hitting and not stopping until you won or dropped dead, and the other side would do the same thing.

In the warehouse, Tyler played Berzerker. The demons came in a swarm like wasps, and Tyler all but closed his eyes and just fought his way forward. The sword was powerful; the demons were only half-solid. Their only real advantage was in their numbers. Their presence darkened the warehouse so that Tyler felt he was fighting through a cloud, a thick shadow that made it almost impossible to see anything but eyes and spectral faces, but he knew where he was going, roughly, and he followed Mary's advice in bludgeoning his way to the door.

He reached the exhaust-stained, artifically-lit air of the outside world with a burst of triumph, his body scratched and aching, his face swollen from the punch. He stumbled through the warehouse door and ran for the car, realizing he'd forgotten to get the keys and hoping someone else had them.

And then he stopped.

He was the only one who had made it out.

He waited a few antsy seconds and then went back through the door. From the outside of the demonic cloud he could see a little more clearly, so the centre of the attack was visible.

The others hadn't moved.

Angelica was standing over Tony, and Mary was standing over Richard, and Tyler knew in a rush that they weren't going to move. Either they were taking their unconscious friends with them, or they would all die together.

He couldn't see Chris.

For some reason his eyes were drawn to the floor, and it seemed the thirty feet between him and the others closed up and he could see as though he were standing right there. Richard's eyes were opening. He was staring up at the ceiling . . .

. . . or at something else high up there.

And Tyler heard his voice, rasping and coming with effort but coming nevertheless.

"Reese," he said, "get out of here!"

Tyler looked up. Reese was there, frozen on the iron stairway coming down from the catwalk above. The look on her face was stricken.

And then she jumped.

And landed on David, taking him down to the ground.

The attack momentarily eased away from the Oneness on the floor.

Reese's sword was drawn, white-hot, and she was holding its point in the hollow of David's throat.

*   *   *   *   *

Reese stared down into the man's face, lit by the heat of her own sword—a sword that could kill him, for he was Oneness, and Oneness was supernatural and vulnerable to the weapons of the Spirit.

Richard's words sledgehammered at her soul.

Get out of here.

Go.

All the grief of rejection rose up in her throat and choked her, and almost blind with it, she pressed the sword farther.

She was dimly aware that the battle had paused, drawn back to watch—that her grief was, for the moment, the focal point of the war.

She stared into the face of a man she had trusted and followed for most of her life. A man who had done more than slander her—who had projected onto her the darkest, most hidden parts of his own soul so that no one could see who she was, so that those she loved distrusted and rejected her, so that she was made to carry the weight of guilt for the death of a friend and to see herself as the enemy of all that she loved, of all that she was.

Her eyes blurred with tears. She did not move the sword.

Richard was saying something . . . trying to yell something at her. She couldn't discern the words.

"It will save them all," David croaked. "If you kill me."

It was true, wasn't it? It wasn't revenge—it was the only thing to do. Without David's leadership the core would lose its power. The hive would eventually disintegrate, losing the unity they needed to function together. In the moment, his death would lend her friends the strength to survive, confusing their enemies badly enough to allow them to fight their way free.

There wasn't even an inch between them and freedom.

Tears ran down her face. Feebly, she tried to reach out for Oneness—to feel the companionship, the faith, the unity with the others that was her greatest strength. To feel the love that bound them all together.

She could feel nothing but the almost physical pain of exile.

"Reese," she finally heard Richard say. "This is not the way."

Rachel Starr Thomson

She closed her eyes, desperately trying to find some semblance of clarity—the conviction needed to stop herself from killing David in what she knew, deep down, would be nothing more than a desperate attempt to set herself free.

Maybe it would work.

After all, he was the cause of all this, and untold other pain. He had killed the hermit, had nearly killed April, had fractured a cell.

Justice had to be done.

Didn't it?

Eyes still closed, she saw a woman's face.

Diane.

And slowly, she backed away.

She pulled the sword tip back. The blade cooled and then vanished. She pushed herself off her knees, off David's chest, and reached her hand out to him.

His eyes went black with madness, and he spat at her hand.

"There is no exile, David," she said. "Not me, and not you. Love holds the Oneness together. And love does not give up on anyone."

She turned and faced the cloud of demonic beings hovering in waiting. The sword reappeared in her hand.

"We are here," she announced. "And we are not running."

The sword heated white. Across the warehouse floor, the swords of her companions did the same. Richard was crouched, sword in hand, smiling, swaying in his physical weakness but ready to fight as much as he could. In the doorway, Tyler stood with his feet apart, sword ready.

Reese looked across the entire warehouse to Chris, who had hidden himself in a corner away from the fight he could have no part in, and smiled.

The demons shrieked and threw themselves back into the fight.

But David ran, and some of the demons followed.

The core, fractured, shook with confusion.

They fought.

But the Oneness was stronger.

* * * * *

"Well," Diane said slowly, turning around and around with the torch held high. "You do have eyes to see, don't you?"

It was early morning. She had driven out here hours after Reese and Chris left the village, following the one thing Reese had told her that she felt courage enough to face.

It had taken her hours, but she'd finally found the cave.

The rock painting took on shadows and dimensions in the torchlight. In two places, figures stood out. One was a man wreathed in darkness, shadows going out from him like rays from an anti-sun. As they went out from him, they took on the shapes of demons and then of other men and women with their eyes lit by evil. The detail was incredible.

The other was Reese, standing in the centre of a battle. Smiling.

Victory seen and painted ahead of time.

Diane set the torch down, leaning it against a crop of rock on the floor, and gingerly lifted April's head and shoulders, trying to administer water from a flask. It dribbled out—April couldn't respond even involuntarily. Not surprising. It was Sunday; she'd been three full days and three full nights without food or water. And was injured besides.

Clucking softly, Diane put out the torch and set all her attention to picking April up. The girl was small and she was lighter than Diane expected.

"I've got an IV in the car," Diane explained. "You're coming home with me, and you're going to be all right in no time."

To her surprise and delight, April stirred in her arms.

"That's right," Diane said. "You're coming home."

Diane stepped into the sunlight with April in her arms. The bay glistened far below. A strong sense of peace, of rightness, pressed down with the warmth of the sun.

Diane did not put words to what she knew.

That she too, for the first time in twenty years, was truly going home.

The End

The story of the Oneness continues in Book 2: *The Hive*.

Rachel would love to hear from you!

You can visit her and interact online:
Web: www.rachelstarrthomson.com
Facebook: www.facebook.com/RachelStarrThomsonWriter
Twitter: @writerstarr

The Seventh World Trilogy

Worlds Unseen   Burning Light   Coming Day

For five hundred years the Seventh World has been ruled by a tyrannical empire—and the mysterious Order of the Spider that hides in its shadow. History and truth are deliberately buried, the beauty and treachery of the past remembered only by wandering Gypsies, persecuted scholars, and a few unusual seekers. But the past matters, as Maggie Sheffield soon finds out. It matters because its forces will soon return and claim lordship over her world, for good or evil.

The Seventh World Trilogy is an epic fantasy, beautiful, terrifying, pointing to the realities just beyond the world we see.

"An excellent read, solidly recommended for fantasy readers."
– Midwest Book Review

"A wonderfully realistic fantasy world. Recommended."
– Jill Williamson, Christy-Award-Winning Author
of *By Darkness Hid*

"Epic, beautiful, well-written fantasy that sings of Christian truth."
– Rael, reader

Available everywhere online or special order from your local bookstore.

The Oneness Cycle

  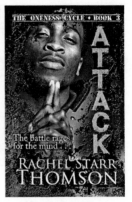

Exile   Hive   Attack

Coming Soon: Renegade and Rise

The supernatural entity called the Oneness holds the world together. What happens if it falls apart?

When Tyler fishes the girl out of the bay, he thinks she's dead. She wishes she was. For Reese, life ended when the the Oneness threw her out. For Tyler, dredging Reese out of the water means life is nothing he thought. In a world where the Oneness exists, nothing looks the same. Dead men walk. Demons prowl the air. Old friends peel back their mundane masks and prove as supernatural as angels. But after centuries of battling demons and the corrupting powers of the world, the Oneness is under a new threat—its greatest threat. Because this time, the threat comes from within.

Fast-paced contemporary fantasy.

"Plot twists and lots of edge-of-your-seat action, I had a hard time putting it down! Waiting with great anticipation for the next in the series."

—Alexis

"I sped through this short, fast-paced novel, pleased by the well-drawn characters and the surprising plot. Thomson has done a great job of portraying difficult emotional journeys . . . Read it!"

—Phyllis Wheeler, The Christian Fantasy Review

Available everywhere online or special order from your local bookstore.

Novels by Rachel Starr Thomson

TAERITH

"Devastatingly beautiful" . . . *"Deeply satisfying."*

LADY MOON

"Laugh-out-loud funny"

*"Reminiscent of Patricia C. Wrede and
Terry Brooks's Magic Kingdom for Sale."*

REAP THE WHIRLWIND

"Haunting."

THEODORE PHARRIS SAVES THE UNIVERSE

"Imaginative and hilarious."

*Available everywhere online
or special order from your local bookstore!*

Short Fiction by Rachel Starr Thomson

BUTTERFLIES DANCING

FALLEN STAR

OF MEN AND BONES

OGRES IS

JOURNEY

MAGDALENE

THE CITY CAME CREEPING

WAYFARER'S DREAM

WAR WITH THE MUSE

SHIELDS OF THE EARTH

And more!

Available as downloads for
Kindle, Kobo, Nook, iPad, and more!

CPSIA information can be obtained
at www.ICGtesting.com
Printed in the USA
FSOW02n0415091216
28166FS